GOTCHA!
THE LAST DAYS OF BLUEFISH (SSN-645)

GOTCHA!
THE LAST DAYS OF BLUEFISH (SSN-645)

BY
Samuel Báez

This is a work of fiction. Any resemblance to real persons, circumstances, or events is purely coincidental.

Cover design by Sheila Hart Design, Inc.

FIRST EDITION
All rights reserved, including the right of reproduction in whole or in part in any form.
Copyright © 2013 by Samuel Báez

Published by Leon Books
19 Riverside Dr.
Waterford, Ct. 06385

Manufactured in the United States of America

ISBN: 978-1492774310
Library of Congress Catalog Card No: 2012902825

0 9 8 7 6 5 4 3 2 1 0

DEDICATION

This book is dedicated to those who treat creation with equity and justice, helping make the universe and our planet, Earth, as wonderful as it should be. It is also dedicated to every person who can believe that PEACE is not something to see happen in the future, but that can be achieved with one another, a moment at a time.

Chapter One	1
Chapter Two	7
Chapter Three	10
Chapter Four	14
Chapter Five	23
Chapter Six	27
Chapter Seven	32
Chapter Eight	36
Chapter Nine	38
Chapter Ten	42
Chapter Eleven	48
Chapter Twelve	53
Chapter Thirteen	60
Chapter Fourteen	67
Chapter Fifteen	76
Chapter Sixteen	83
Chapter Seventeen	86
Chapter Eighteen	92
Chapter Nineteen	102
Chapter Twenty	109
Chapter Twenty-One	114
Chapter Twenty-Two	122
Chapter Twenty-Three	124
Chapter Twenty-Four	127
Chapter Twenty-Five	131

GOTCHA!
THE LAST DAYS OF BLUEFISH (SSN-645)

CHAPTER ONE

IT WAS 1700 HOURS. Twilight was just beginning to fade. Phil was forcing himself not to look back at the submarine. The gold braid, or "scrambled eggs," on his commander's hat looked impressive. So did the two rows of ribbons on his chest. The gold dolphins, insignia of submarine officers, glistened as the overhead floodlights hit them. The command pin showing he was the "skipper" of USS *Bluefish* (SSN-645), a fast attack submarine, dominated the uniform below the left breast pocket of his Blues.

As he sloshed through the January ice and snow, making his way from the sub mooring, Commander Phillip E. Blair, United States Navy, thought, "Damn, this is an un-colorful way to go!" He and his crew were in the midst of an in-activation evolution. The reality of his lifelong dream, the command of a sub—this one, one of the best—a 637 Sturgeon class—was about to end. *Bluefish* and its crew could not have performed better!

He walked away from it toward an official white sedan assigned by the squadron. The Navy seal bearing a proud eagle with wings outstretched had been removed. Both the seal and the following words, "US Navy, United States of America," had always made him stand taller. The words were still visibly emblazoned on both front doors. Now the letters "USN" followed by a long identification number appeared but did nothing for the rich heritage the men in navy blue represented. Perhaps the powers that be thought keeping a low profile for the taxpayers was important.

The driver, chilled by the unusually biting cold day in southeastern Connecticut, shifted from one foot to the other. He slapped his sides with glove-covered hands. As the *Bluefish*'s captain approached, the enlisted sailor saluted and greeted him respectfully, "Evening, captain, sir!"

"Evening, sailor," was the subdued reply. He returned the salute. His downcast mood kept him from making his salute and greeting as sharp as he normally liked. He slid into the back seat, reached for his cover and slammed it down beside him. The door closed and the driver accelerated the engine, which had been idling, to force more warm air into the now-occupied vehicle.

Phil looked through the clouded back window. His mind quickly reviewed his orders to in-activate "his" sub. As he did so, he thought, "This might be the beginning of the end of this submarine, but by Jesus, 'my crew'," and he swallowed as he thought of each one of them. All those fine officers and men who are *Bluefish*—"all of them are very much alive!"

The last time *Bluefish* had glided into port after a successful patrol was less than a month ago, two days before Christmas. They had intended to arrive a day earlier to follow the official schedule, but Mother Nature had had another plan. The rain had started two days before *Bluefish* was due in New London harbor. A mile down the Thames River due north of the boat's location was the site of the "Largest and Best Submarine Homeport in the World." The high school band set its plan to play at the welcoming ceremony on hold. It was traditional to greet the sailors with as much fanfare as possible when they had been deployed to the North Atlantic or Mediterranean for months at a time. The wives and children, as well as girlfriends and friends, abandoned their long-planned homecoming, which had included banners and noisemakers, when weather predictions sounded gloomy. On the day of the scheduled arrival the State pier area had turned to a glassy sheet of ice. The rain had turned to sleet and the wind made the chill factor a freezing minus twenty degrees. Phil's wife, Estelle, had later told him the roads were treacherous. WSUB at 980 kilocycles from Groton and WNLC at 1510 kilocycles from New London had warned drivers to stay off the roads, especially off the spans of the Gold Star Memorial Bridge linking the two cities. *Bluefish*, heeding the traveler's advisory and, more officially, the orders from Submarine Group 2, headquartered at the lower base, regretfully accepted the delay. They rode out the bulk of the winter storm at sea.

The *Bluefish* was met by two sturdy Navy tugs just beyond Race Point in the Long Island Sound a day after the big winter storm. They pulled alongside and looked like appendages on the slowly moving but effortlessly plying monster fish making its way through the choppy waters of the Thames River. The line handlers on the tugs, most of whom were female sailors with the aid of the sub sailors, quickly attached each craft and moved toward land. The submarine crew had been readying the boat at sea. There was little to do except tie her up and go on liberty for most of those on board. From past experience, they knew it wouldn't take more than a few hours for everyone to get back to homeport routine. The knowledge that this would be the last time *Bluefish* would come in from patrol was shared by all. As far as they were concerned, this was the end of the line for their home away from home.

As *Bluefish*'s commanding officer continued to peer out the partially frosted window of the sedan, he couldn't help but think of the "trusty old gal" which, in spite of its twenty-five years of service, had been a damn good ship.

He recalled the day he had taken command. The squadron commander had congratulated him on being the *Bluefish*'s ninth commanding officer. He was reminded of its past, including how it had been given the same name as a previous sub that had sunk ten enemy vessels totaling thousands of tons. Meritorious Unit Commendations and other awards for overall battle efficiency were part of its past honored history to the present.

His two years aboard had gone fast. Again, he thought to himself that the *real* story behind the *real* ship were the men in *Bluefish*'s history. Without them, without their ups and downs and their ability to sail in spite of great sacrifice, *Bluefish* would never have made its many dives, patrolled the ocean lanes or engaged in dangerous patrols. One very historic patrol stood out to him. Perhaps that was because it ended up risking the lives of all aboard.

...

Each moment of that patrol was etched in his memory. It came back to him like a flash of light.

...

The sleek-looking, fast attack nuclear sub, *Bluefish* (SSN-645), which he commanded was quietly gliding SSW at four hundred feet at a comfortable eighteen knots. He remembered that its six-month deployment in the North Atlantic, where he and his crew had been keeping track of the former Soviet Union's submarine movements, was nearly over. His crew was looking forward to one last liberty. More importantly, the 112 or more enlisted men and ten officers were finally headed for the good old U.S.A. Making love would again be a reality!

Radioman First Class Jeff Harvey had ripped a message from the computer printer. It read:

TOP SECRET
Abort present mission. Proceed Longitude 75 degrees W. Latitude 15 degrees N. CIA tracking freighter heading U.S. port. Suspect illegal drug cargo. Intercept.
OP-02 0800 Zulu

This didn't make any sense. The latest orders they had from Washington absolutely forbade any military interdiction, other than what was being used, in the "War on Drugs." What could have changed? The Navy had been used to help recover planes downed in the oceans, or to pick up survivors or refugees, but this? Phil's executive officer then, Lieutenant Commander Herman "Pappy" Brown, a top performer and rising star, discussed the message with him. For years they had known only the routine mission for subs, which was "detecting, tracking and destroying enemy surface ships and submarines." Now they were being asked to change their modus operandi to "intercepting a freighter with illegal drugs." Brown and he tried to make sense of this when another message from Submarine Headquarters appeared on the radio room computer printer. It read:

TOP SECRET
Surveillance by CIA spy satellite now verifies previous information. Proceed as ordered. Use extreme caution.
OP-02 1000 Zulu.

All department heads joined the XO and CO in the wardroom at the skipper's order. They gazed at one another as the messages were passed around. Their quizzical looks reflected the same question that had been on the mind of the two senior officers...*a US submarine involved in the interdiction of illegal drugs on the high seas?*

Blair and the rest of the wardroom were all aware of the US Coast Guard's role in intercepting and searching vessels and arresting personnel aboard those boats who were suspected of trafficking in drugs inside the US authorized territorial limits of ocean lanes. In addition, they knew that Navy vessels had been carrying Coast Guard personnel to make searches of suspicious boats and cargo. "Operation Blast Furnace" had used Army Special Forces and an airborne unit in Bolivia to wipe out thousands of acres of a marijuana crop. Local gendarmes were also involved. The Drug Enforcement Administration (DEA) had made it known that vigilance at the US borders, especially along Mexico and deep inside that country, was to increase. Para-military groups in foreign countries were making a steady inroad into discovering drug cartels across the world. The president had given up on using the DEA and the

US Armed Forces in Peru, largest coca leaf grower in the world. The "Sendero Luminoso" (Shining Path)—clever terrorists who were committed to the protection of producers and runners of drugs in Peru—posed a threat to US lives. Advisors to Colombia and Bolivia were being sent to try to figure out how to stem this cancer. The American public was still too hesitant to send their young sons to another Vietnam only to be slaughtered by well-armed guerillas. Protecting America's oil trade with the Near East had given the president's executive order authority to send over 500,000 troops in concert with U.N. Resolutions and support, as well as the US Congress's consent. The department heads in the wardroom thought, "The Armed Forces might lend humanitarian assistance to Somalia's starving millions, but certainly the strategy to use submarines to keep drugs out of American soil seems like an incredible approach. No way!"

Lieutenant Clifford Brandish, the weapons department head, had commented, "What the hell's going on? We're still supposed to be tracking subs. The Pentagon's gone out of its gourd!"

Another, newly promoted lieutenant commander, Blake P. Summers, engineering department head and an older officer, had volunteered, "This is no job for us. How can we do anything in international waters? What do you think we're going to be expected to do? Maybe it's one of our freighters and the Pentagon has made a mistake."

The comments continued: "Someone's got to be kidding! Who would take a chance like that? I bet we'll find it to be a foreign ship we can't touch. In spite of *glasnost*, you can never be too sure of what even the so-called 'commonwealth of Independent States' is up to these days. I, personally, go along with 'trust, but verify.'"

A deep silence seemed to pervade the small room filled with the ten most senior leaders of the *Bluefish*'s crew. The quiet was broken only by the smooth hum of the nuclear-powered engines.

CHAPTER TWO

THE THOUGHTS OF THE MEN in the wardroom bounced back and forth. They knew that, at this moment, there was no answer to the illicit drug problem at either end, source or demand. The politicians and educators had tried as well, with no scent of a solution.

Some politicians had said: "Send troops to Peru or Bolivia or Colombia or Mexico...let's get at the source. Just wipe out the fields, the elicit production sources, and eliminate the drug lords. The U.S.A. has plenty of ammo to wipe 'em off the face of the earth. Use defoliates, burn the sons o' bitches. No mercy."

Others had been saying education was the answer: "We've got to start with our pre-schoolers and elementary level youngsters. In one or two generations, they'll learn to say 'no' to drugs, having learned the facts about drugs and the repercussions of abuse."

A few had proposed that both approaches needed to be used, but both the sources of drugs and their use kept increasing. The cancer was spreading as each day dawned.

...

The ten officers drew a deep breath as they agreed there was a need to be united against the enemy who was hitting at the most vulnerable level of American society: the young and impressionable. The skirmishes that had been fought on different fronts in the previous wars on drugs had failed to stem drug availability. Drug addiction had become a national plague.

"Somebody is finally recognizing that this is 'war.'"

"Our kids are the ones being slowly massacred."

"Thank God we're beginning to fight fire with fire."

"We've got to remember our kids are the life-blood of our nation's and the world's future."

...

The skipper thought of his own son, now fourteen. He and the rest of the officers, and at least half of the crew, were parents. Captain Blair ordered his department heads, "Tell your men we are now heading into Caribbean waters." He was sure the crew would approve this sudden change of assignments.

Though they had been looking forward to getting home after a long and somewhat boring patrol, a feeling of excitement seemed to hit the crew as the department heads each went back to their respective sections. They all seemed to get their second wind in a hurry.

The systems all began to get the close look every submariner gives his boat. All hand weapons and the principal weapons of the SSN, the nuclear head and conventional head torpedoes, were checked carefully once again. Ensign Jonathan Palmer, the most junior officer who had been aboard the shortest time, mused, "Damn, this is better than just saying 'no.' Somebody's finally started facing reality!"

...

Captain Blair continued remembering that as *Bluefish* was then making its way between the Florida Keys and Cuba, heading SW, a routine intercom message came into the XO's stateroom. Upon hearing it he reported to the captain, "Just got a message from Lieutenant Valdez in engineering. One of our men is vomiting. Seems pretty bad, he says."

"Who's the man?" asked the concerned skipper, who was known for his personal approach to everyone aboard.

"Engineman First Class Otto Turner," XO answered. "Valdez said he had complained of a splitting headache just moments before."

"Make sure he gets to sick bay right away!" ordered the CO.

As he said that, Hospital Corpsman First Class Erik Amundsen, or "Doc," as he was known to everyone, burst into the captain's stateroom. "Just saw Turner, sir," he said. "His fever is going over 104 degrees. Doesn't look good to me."

"You look worried!"

"He looks bad. Better get back to him."

As Amundsen sped away, the CO called out, "Good man, Amundsen. Do your best."

"Yeah, 'Doc,' keep a close watch!" echoed the XO.

EM1 Turner was in bad shape. Amundsen and Valdez applied cold compresses all over his feverish body. In spite of that, Turner began convulsing. His pulse was speeding up. His blood pressure continued climbing. Valdez called the CO. The XO took off for Sick Bay!

...

The radio room was receiving another message:

TOP SECRET

Identity of freighter, "Panamanian." Execute as ordered. Will advise action. OP-02 1200 Zulu

---

The executive officer broke into the CO's stateroom without announcement. CO had just finished a cup of coffee after reading the message. He was furiously pounding his desk.

"Those dirty bastards!" Lieutenant Commander Brown said. His face had lost all its color. In fact, he looked like death warmed over.

CO could only guess but he asked, hoping for the best, "What's the word on Turner?"

XO could hardly speak. His eyes welled up with tears. "...He's dead!"

Grimacing and running his hand through a prematurely balding head, the CO put his hand on Brown's shoulder and, in a moment of shock, he asked almost in a whisper, "What the hell are we supposed to do now?"

CHAPTER THREE

THE CAPTAIN KNEW THAT a dead crewmember aboard an operating submarine, especially one on patrol, required special attention. A choice would have to be made. It was a decision Phil Blair would have to make alone.

"Can you believe this is happening to us, Pappy?"

Before Pappy could answer, LCDR Summer had joined them from engineering. He broke in, "CO, Turner has a wife and two children back in Groton. We've got to get him back! Can't we tell the Pentagon what's happened and forget this whole 'freighter' bit?"

"Wish it was that easy, Blake! I've got to give this some thought. Make sure Turner's body is prepared and put into the reefer. We'll let the crew know what's going on after I decide what to do." He rounded up his department heads and, together with the XO, they all discussed the dilemma facing them. Everyone had a different opinion. They all agreed they were glad they weren't the final decision maker. It was up to the captain!

The captain felt the loneliness of command. He excused himself from the wardroom, but as he walked through the hatch into the passageway, he said, "Give me fifteen minutes, alone. I'll have the answer."

...

Years ago, there would have been no choice. The mission would have taken priority. In a way, it was easier then, if it ever is easier to keep a dead crewmember aboard for any reason.

In the past, when a boat returned from deployment and was met by the band and cheering wives and children, parents or girlfriends, there was always a very real possibility that someone would be carried across the bow in a flag-draped stretcher on the way to the morgue. It was one of the unspoken fears of the families.

With the Cold War now over, it was no longer necessary to keep such tight security. A new relationship had made the US the only superpower and the threat of hostilities came only from possible terrorist Third World states.

The strategy for surfacing had varied amongst commanding officers of the nuclear submarine fleet. It was all part of the big game. At one time, keeping "the enemy" guessing was important. The War College and CO and XO grooming school had pounded this into their heads before they went on to command their ship.

If it was known that a patrol had been aborted, the immediate question by any spying power, whether by satellite or other means, was "Why?" There were many possibilities the potential adversaries could play with, among them: possible problems with the power supply or other systems; a broken and dangerous part requiring immediate repair, which couldn't be done by personnel on board; orders from higher headquarters for international reasons; or, a serious illness of one of the crewmembers. The possibility that a submarine would feign being "wounded" was another strategy that would bring out a second sub to relieve it.

Captain Blair knew that he could put an end to the orders from the Pentagon by surfacing and using the return of EM1 Turner's body home as an excuse for aborting the new mission. Aborting the patrol was one thing, but aborting the new mission didn't sit well with the skipper. He couldn't make a rash decision. He sat at his tiny desk, knowing he was responsible for the total crew, as well as a $21 million weapon system. At age thirty-six, he was feeling like an old man.

As he sat there wondering what to do, memories of his having taken command of *Bluefish* flashed through his mind.

...

He and his crew had manned one of thousands of ships that plied the oceans under the Stars and Stripes.

Captain Blair thought of his family as he pondered the immediate and the long range future. Commander Phillip E. Blair's father had been Vice Admiral Richard Blair. As one of the Navy's youngest admirals, he had a fine record and was assigned the awesome job of heading the Pacific Task Force against the Japanese at Midway. He was now retired and lived in Essex, Connecticut, just twenty-five miles from New London, with his wife, Jean, happily married for fifty-six years. Phil's oldest brother had died at Inchon, Korea, during that bloody "police action." He knew that his loss among the over fifty-six thousand lost lives of men and women was diminished by such a reference. Their daughter, Lynn, was married to a Coast Guard officer, David—now a captain in Washington, D.C. Phil and his wife, Estelle, were staunch members of their community. Phil hoped that his son, Jim, would pull out of his teenage years without a lot of grief for everyone.

Just before Phil's mind went back into recall, he asked himself, "I wonder where the detailer in Washington will make my next assignment?" He hoped his seniors in Norfolk and elsewhere would speak well of him. As he agonized and hoped, in these ten minutes that seemed like hours, he wished he could see into a crystal ball. His thoughts were interrupted by the "click click" of the computer printing out a message in the nearby radio room. He couldn't escape being on the sub in the middle of the Caribbean. When he got the message, it read:

TOP SECRET
Search, seize, and arrest crew "Panamanian" freighter.
Expect hostilities. Cargo, drugs. OP-02 1300 Zulu

Now Blair knew that not only were Submarine Headquarters and the whole Department of Defense behind this, but so were the Department of Justice, the Congress and the president of the United States. Foreign policy, not just national law enforcement, was at stake. The American people were behind this new and daring "War on Drugs." He sensed it could be an all out war. He had five minutes to go before his final decision. He reviewed the alternatives.

...

"What if the freighter is armed with missiles?" he asked himself "They could wipe us out! No one would know of Turner's death." He had to take that risk! "My guess is, they will look for a fight. I doubt they'll surrender that easily."

There was a minute left in his self-imposed fifteen-minute deadline. In those sixty seconds, he reached for the unused Bible on the shelf above his desk. His father had told him he might need it someday. In desperation, he opened it and closed his eyes in a prayer gesture. The only word he could muster was "Help!" When he opened his eyes, he knew what to do.

"Blessed are the peacemakers" were the words that seemed to force themselves out of the page, and that was all he needed to recall that the Submarine Force prided itself in the motto, "A Deterrent Force for Peace."

CHAPTER FOUR

A SLIGHT SMILE COULD BE SEEN on the skipper's visibly relaxed, though aging, face as he went into the wardroom. The informality they shared kept the men seated as he came in, though they wanted to stand to receive his official word. Each utterance came out clearly. Never before had the officers been more respectful and awed by his presence. They knew at that moment, more than ever, that he was in charge.

In an authoritative and decisive voice he said, "The mission Washington has expected us to perform is on!" There was confidence in every syllable. "Turner's body will be returned in a timely manner, as well. Make no mistake about that!

"As important, and now perhaps, more so, is the future! We on *Bluefish* can make history. We must not fail our country. The freighter will be stopped!"

The officers looked at each other. They yearned to join together in a cheer echoing the sentiments of the American people—that our children deserve a drug-free environment. They slapped each other on the back rather than let out the loud cheer they would have preferred. The CO recognized that they went along with his decision and were in a mood for celebration.

"We'll go down fighting if we have to, but we're in a hell'uva good position to do something about this murderous scheme that's killing our kids. Let's get on with it!"

...

He got on the boat's IMC.

"Men, this is the captain speaking. We are approaching possible hostilities. As some of you have heard already, Washington has ordered us to abort what was the end of our patrol in the North Atlantic. We were on the way back home and were going to make one last liberty port call in Keflavick, Iceland. That was scrapped, and now we are deep into Caribbean waters.

"A suspected 'Panamanian' freighter carrying drugs is on its way to a US port. The Pentagon wants us to intercept, search, and if they're right about the drugs, we're to arrest the crew. We've got to prepare for anything!

"If I have anything to say about it, *Bluefish* is going to be successful. We are about to make history and our involvement may record this action as *the* turning point in the *war* against drugs."

"You are aware of EM1 Turner's death. We have lost one of our top shipmates. His body will be returned to port in the appropriate manner at the appropriate time. He, as the father of two little girls, would want us to take up America's 'call to arms.'"

...

EM1 Turner had been one of the most popular members of *Bluefish*'s crew. He was also the most decorated. His membership in the Armed Forces had included hitches in the Army and the Marine Corps. For the last ten years, he'd been in the Navy, mostly on *Bluefish*. He had looked forward to retirement at the end of this patrol. He had nearly twenty-two years of service to his country.

The last eight years on *Bluefish* had seen Otto go through the pipeline as engineman until his death, leading petty officer in the Nuclear Reactor Section of the Engineering Department. In addition, he was depended on for his knowledge of the back-up diesel system to the nuclear power. His expertise had been responsible for helping *Bluefish* pass all of its exams and tests by the squadron with flying colors. The coveted Battle Efficiency Pennant, Navy Unit Commendation, and Meritorious Unit Commendations with gold stars had been won by *Bluefish* during his lifetime aboard. EM1 Turner had been an integral part of uniting the crew in their successful efforts.

Among his many talents, he was a cartoonist, and he added pleasure and humor to the boat's plan of the day, called the "POD" by the crew. He had caricatured every man at one point, adding a brief biography plus a personal interview narrative to the POD. All of these PODs, with their recollection of *Bluefish*'s crew, would later be made into a book in Turner's memory.

Turner's first wife had died following a tragic automobile accident in which their only child, Lance, had also been killed. Otto had been married to Becky now for eleven years.

Before his last patrol, Becky and Otto and their two children, Orlinda (ten), born in Orlando, Florida, and Debby (eight), born in Groton, were sitting around the kitchen table in their Trident Park home in Navy housing in Groton.

"Why don't we make a down payment on that house in Gales Ferry?" asked Becky for what seemed the thousandth time.

"We just don't have the money. Even though you're a nurse, and have a good job, we're just barely making it," Otto had replied, scratching his head.

What Otto did not know was that Becky had been saving money each payday and now had accumulated nearly $3,000 in ten years.

"Mommy, it would be nice to have our own house. We keep moving from one place to another all the time. I'm only ten and we've moved every two years—that's five times," said Orlinda.

"Yeah," chimed in Debby, "and my Teddy and other toys would be safe."

As in most close neighborhoods, it was hard to keep the children in control, and there had been some stealing. They have moved from Dolphin Gardens to Nautilus Park and now to Trident Park. Each place had been a little better, but still not their own. After Orlando they had been in all the Navy housing units in Groton, except Polaris Park.

Becky had vowed years ago to keep her savings secret to herself. She had wanted to surprise Otto.

After supper that evening, Otto and Becky had gone on one of those rare nights out without the children. A wife of a deployed sailor from another submarine came to baby-sit. They had gone to a movie. On the way back, they reminisced about the past, still wishing they were going back to their own house. As Otto drove, his hand reached over and warmly covered Becky's. She slid over toward him and snuggled her face in his strong shoulder.

"Wouldn't our folks be proud of us if we had our own place for them to visit? It would be much nicer," coaxed Becky, pleading with all the love her eyes could muster.

"But, even with a G.I. Loan, it would be tough. The payments would be too high each month even if we don't need a down payment that way," said Otto with some hesitation. Both of them were conservative spenders, but Becky knew about her secret savings.

"I was going to wait until later, but I've got to tell you now. I've been saving some money, Otto."

"What are you talking about?"

"I have $3,000 at home."

"You *what?*"

"I couldn't tell you. It was supposed to be a surprise for when we decided on buying a house."

"Well, that makes a big difference." Still sounding a bit shocked, Otto declared, "You know that does put a new light on things."

Becky, delighted at his response, snuggled even closer. "While you're out on this next patrol, I'll look around real carefully. I'll pick out a place within our price range. It'll be good to have a place we can move to when you retire. I can work more, you'll have another job, and with those two incomes plus your pension you're getting from the Navy, we'll be able to swing it."

"Let's not tell the kids, yet. We'll wait 'til I get back, okay, Hon?" He rarely used endearing terms. She knew he meant it!

Turner had come from Duluth, Minnesota; Becky from Baraboo, Wisconsin. When Otto's first wife died along with his son, he had vowed never to marry again. But as fortune would have it, a year later he ran across Becky, whom he had met at a church camp years earlier. Becky had never married. She was to be the best thing that happened to Otto to help him get beyond his grief and loneliness. He insisted that he couldn't marry but Becky couldn't be denied. A year later they tied the knot.

A first generation, US citizen who prided himself on being German and English, Otto was quick to accept one of the responsibilities of citizenship: that of serving his country. After high school he was drafted into the Army, fought in Vietnam and was released to the cruel world of post-Vietnam. No one was interested in a "blood-thirsty" veteran. He needed to support his new wife. The Marine Corps enlisted him as a corporal (E-4). When he made staff sergeant (E-6) he heard of an inter-service transfer and was brought into the Navy as an (E-6), a first class. He had only been married to Sarah three years, and their son was one and one-half years old when that tragic automobile accident happened.

When he and Becky married, she went with him to the EM "A" school and nuclear power school in Orlando, Florida. It seemed appropriate to name their first child after what they thought was a honeymoon assignment near Disney World.

While at the Prototype in Windsor Locks, Connecticut, Debby was born. The assignment to *Bluefish* had kept them in the Groton, New London area. His inability to make chief (E-7) was based on difficulties in taking tests. Through tutoring, he had been able to pass the last test and was awaiting promotion.

...

At the request of Commander Blair, the yeoman chief in admin had given Phil all the biographical information on EM1Turner. A eulogy would have to be prepared. Turner's department head, Lieutenant Commander Blake Summer, the XO, and CO compared notes. They all knew the special attention that had to be given to a dead crewmember of a sub on patrol. The choice would be left to the commanding officer.

"You and I are about to become peacemakers for millions of Americans and children in particular." He added, in a tone that revealed his personal feelings, "I know you're all in agreement that there should be an end to the drug lords. They and others are making money on the young, those so easily influenced. Some of them are your brothers and sisters. I don't have to explain to you how others in our society are affected by this blight. We cannot minimize the fact that we have lost a top shipmate in EM1 Turner. He, I believe, as a father of two little girls, would not want us to abort this secret mission. Good luck and God bless you!"

Those who had known of Washington's new mission for the *Bluefish*, and had thought it should not take precedence over returning EM1 Turner's body, were relieved by their captain's decision. They seemed to feel strength in his reliance on a Higher Power. The mood of the whole crew was upbeat.

...

As the ship's horn sounded—calling 'All hands to battle stations!'—*THE ENTIRE CREW MOVED AS ONE!* They, to a man, had heard the skipper. Even those in their racks jumped out of their spaces, got dressed, and reported to their sections. *THE ADRENALIN WAS FLOWING!*

...

The ship's inertial navigation system (SINS), which gave them their bearings, called off *Bluefish*'s exact location every fifteen seconds. The control room was bustling as speeds and directions were being coordinated with Engineering.

Now just miles from their destination, the sonar gear detected a large ship. "Echoes indicate movement of a large object twenty degrees off port bow moving at fifteen knots!" called Sonarman First Class Clement Johnson to the control room duty officer. Jackson was *Bluefish*'s only African American. Years ago, an admiral had stood in the wardroom of the tender and said, "The US Submarine Force is too white!" Jackson was a breath of fresh air. He stood in a proud line of blacks, though too few, who had served their country faithfully. Since the birth of the Silent Service in 1911 there had been too few, indeed.

...

From a depth of one hundred fifty feet, the captain ordered, "Surface to periscope depth!" The planes-men, two of the newest crewmembers, followed the diving officer's orders, which came as a response to their skipper's. "Periscope depth, aye!" they said.

The instrument panel showed that *Bluefish* was on its way up. Men on their way to their battle stations, in the passageway, adjusted their balance. *Bluefish*'s periscope broke the surface one thousand yards from the freighter. The large craft had not spotted the sub. *Bluefish* approached on their starboard side.

...

As part of the plan, Electronic Technician Third Class, Francisco Calderón, or "Cisco" as the crew knew him, had been briefed thoroughly about the mission. ET3 Calderón was of Spanish extraction, born in El Paso, Texas, of immigrant parents. CO and XO had sensed that having bilingual members of the crew was of utmost importance, especially in the Navy's tasks with the Coast Guard.

At twenty, Cisco was the oldest of four. Johnny (thirteen), Robby (eleven) and Armenia (nine) made up the rest of the Calderón clan. Their parents, Rudolfo, a mail carrier back in Texas, and Teresa, a beauty operator, had done well with their brood. Cisco had barely escaped the drug scene by joining the Navy. He knew that their no-tolerance approach saved him. He wasn't sure how his little brothers and sister would fare. Schools and neighborhoods in El Paso were prime targets for the sleazy, money-grabbing pushers who snuck around like vultures, ready to pounce on innocent victims.

XO spoke to Calderón with respect. He was depending on his bilingual abilities. "You're a key person in this operation, Calderón!"

No more would he be forced to take a ribbing from some of his shipmates because of the color of his skin—a golden olive, but still darker than most of the crew. Calderón had a good sense of humor and an excellent self-image. Consequently, he didn't mind the insensitive comments and jokes about his ethnic background. His ruddy complexion and well-groomed mustache lent to his suave Mexican appearance. For the fun of it, he and Cowboy, a good Texas buddy, played "Red Neck" and "Mexican Migrant" roles to the crew's delight. Calderón hoped this assignment would stop that nonsense for good and that his shipmates would no longer kid around.

Now, carbine strapped across his chest, and wearing an additional weapon, a .45 automatic pistol strapped to his cartridge belt around his waist, Calderón and ten others awaited further orders from the captain as they lined up next to the amidships ladder. The Panamanian freighter would be their next destination.

The name *Isla Verde* appeared between the cross-hairs of the periscope. As Commander Blair rotated the smoothly operating hydraulic scope, he elevated the sight to reveal two human forms, one sitting and one standing, in the freighter's pilot house.

...

Dawn had just arrived. The two figures in the pilot house were supposed to be on watch. As would be the case, in cases where little was going on, the scope revealed that one of the men was sleeping, slouched over the panel counter while sitting in what would be the second-in-command's chair; and the other was standing next to the what would be the captain of the freighter's chair. The freighter was obviously on automatic pilot. It was presumed that the rest of the crew, including *Isla Verde*'s skipper, were catching some Zs.

Commander Blair, now somewhat nervous, but confident, spoke to his XO and control officer. They agreed the *Bluefish* had not been detected.

"Prepare to surface."

The echo command from the control officer came loud and clear: "Prepare to surface, aye!" All the instrumentation indicated readiness. The crew was eager to go.

"Surface and maintain five knots."

"Surface and maintain five knots, aye," was the response as an acceptance to the order. Control and Engine Room both checked their instrument panels cautiously. The boarding crew, headed by Cisco, shifted from one foot to the other.

Bluefish broke the surface like a whale coming up for air. It did so quietly, but its size caused huge waves to rise and splash down against the rising superstructure until the sail and planes, and eventually the stern, were all visible above the water. The stern and main body of the sub actually looked like they were unattached.

It was time for the boarding party to move up the ladder. "NOW!" was the command. They scampered up. One of the men put the US flag atop the sail. Commander Blair wanted to make sure *Isla Verde*'s crew knew who was giving them orders.

The CO, the duty officer and Lieutenant Valdez, the only other Spanish-speaking member of the crew, were all on the sub's bridge at the top of the sail. The battery-powered megaphone switch was engaged. The captain called out, "We have orders to intercept! Stop all engines! We are prepared to board you! Stop all engines!" Commander Blair passed the megaphone to Valdez. He called out in Spanish, "¡Alto! ¡Hemos recibido nuestras órdenes! ¡Vamos a embarcarlos! ¡Alto!"

CHAPTER FIVE

THERE WAS A LOUD CHURNING NOISE from the propellers as the twin shafts of the freighter reversed their clockwise revolution. The watch-standers had responded to the orders from the American submarine and both men in the pilot house, now awake and chattering in Spanish, were busy, one speaking to the engine room, the other to *Isla Verde*'s skipper.

Now dead in the water, the nearly six hundred-foot freighter awaited *Bluefish*'s approach. The disheveled captain was now out on deck. He buttoned his fly as he tried to figure out what was going on. They had been caught totally by surprise. He pulled his polo shirt over his head. It was a balmy eight-two degrees out in the middle of the Caribbean. The inside-out polo shirt, an ill-fitting garment, made its way down a bare and heavy belly.

Commander Blair, from the sail of the sub, called out over the megaphone, "We have orders to inspect your cargo."

Calm seas and no breeze made the procedure seem easy. As LT Valdez began to translate, *Isla Verde*'s skipper called out, "I speak English. Come aboard!" Captain Blair put his crew on even more cautious alert. This seemed too easy! By now several crewmen from *Isla Verde* were on its main deck. The side ladder of the freighter was lowered. Cisco and the rest of the *Bluefish* boarding crew had moved across the calm waters from the sub to the freighter in short order, riding in the new hard bottom inflatable brought aboard the sub before the patrol. They climbed their way onto *Isla Verde*'s main deck, their rifles and .45s ready to fire, if necessary.

Below deck on the sub, the crew was tense. They felt powerless. Their lives depended on those above decks who would either out-talk or out-shoot the suspected drug runners. They waited with bated breath.

Cisco pointed his rifle at the skipper of the freighter and began speaking to him in Spanish, "*Capitán, su nombre, país de origen y tipo de carga.*" (Captain, your name, country of birth and nature of cargo.)

Again, the skipper re-iterated, "I speak English. I'm not looking for a fight. There are twenty-five of us." (Later, they would discover twenty-six was the total number of the crew.) "You can see we are not armed. Word has been passed to all to come topside. Whatever you're looking for, please be my guests." He continued speaking to the boarding party as Commander Blair went on board *Isla Verde*. The freighter's skipper had produced a US passport. The name on it was Estéban Muñoz. It showed Gary, Indiana, as home of record. He also showed Cisco a US driver's license from Indiana. He said, "Back in the Hoosier State, my friends call me Steve. My crew is Colombian. They don't speak English."

By now, both ship's captains were face to face. Each crew was behind its skipper. Muñoz made a half attempt to salute and addressed captain Blair, saying, "Captain?..."

Blair did not give his name. "Your cargo. I must inspect it. Those are my orders from Washington!"

"Oh, of course, you can see for yourself. Coffee beans and oil is all we have! If you're looking for drugs, you're going to be disappointed."

LCDR Brown and the CO let Skipper Muñoz and his first mate start below the main deck. Cisco, Cowboy and Jackson followed—training their carbines on the captain and first mate of the suspected drug runner freighter crew. The others were ordered to lie down on the deck, face down, their hands behind their backs. Three *Bluefish* sailors kept their carbines pointed at them while four others began to handcuff them.

As they stepped down below, Commander Blair asked Muñoz, "Why are you flying a Panamanian flag?"

"Captain..." he tried to remember his name.

"Captain Blair."

"Captain Blair, sir," he tried hard to sound respectful. "We are hired to transport what we have by an international organization known as World Commerce Incorporated. They own this ship. I was told they fly whatever flag they want. We painted *Isla Verde* on the hull just hours before we left Colombia's main port. The Panamanian flag is just one of many we carry on board."

As they proceeded down the ladder, and before stepping down to the deck below, Muñoz signaled to his first mate, who had also gone with the search party, to proceed. He told Commander Blair, "I only do as I'm told. No, Carlos?"

The First Mate heard the Spanish from his skipper. "¡*Sí, mi Comandante!*" he said, acknowledging his comment.

"How many decks are there?" questioned Commander Blair.

"Four. Every deck has coffee bean sacks or oil drums."

When they reached the first cargo deck, Muñoz mentioned to Carlos to take down the metal cutters from the bulkhead shelf containing other tools. Cisco cocked his .45. Muñoz quickly interjected, "No need to do that, Mr. Cisco. Carlos just wants to get the cutters to help with your inspection."

Taking no chances, Jackson clicked the magazine into the carbine. Carlos took the cutters and cut the band around one of the gunny sacks bulging with coffee beans. There were hundreds of similar sacks as far as the eye could see.

"There are two other decks like this," Muñoz uttered.

Carlos cut the top of the sack, pushed it over and the beans, shiny as though polished, a deep alizarin crimson in color, spilled out. Carlos bent down again to lift the sack, and more beans piled onto the deck.

Blair's heart sank. "Could the Pentagon and the Department of Justice and Washington and the CIA and the DEA and OP-02 all have made a mistake?" he thought. As they moved on to a second and third sack of beans without finding any evidence of drugs, Commander Blair began to have more doubts. He and the XO looked at each other. Maybe he should have aborted the special mission and taken EM1 Turner's body back to Groton. But they continued their search.

CHAPTER SIX

AS THE DRUG SEARCH aboard *Isla Verde* proceeded, seemingly futile, Carlos was obediently emptying out each sack of coffee beans. Commander Blair motioned to Cisco to cover Muñoz and Carlos more carefully. He thought he sensed someone else in the below deck storage spaces. His peripheral vision had caught what he thought was movement behind the hundreds of sacks of beans.

As Carlos poured out the contents of one of the sacks, there appeared a sack from within. When the XO grabbed the cutters from Carlos and stuck the sharp edge of one blade into the sack, the Colombian marijuana, which they had been told was on board the freighter, began to spill out.

"Just as Washington suspected, CO. We better check some more," advanced the XO.

"You said you have two other decks of these 'coffee sacks,' Mr. Muñoz?" asked the sub captain sarcastically. Muñoz appeared sheepish. On each level they discovered the hidden marijuana. Muñoz and Carlos were now handcuffed.

"What's in these, did you say, Muñoz?" quipped the now-angry *Bluefish* commander.

"I was told, and the shipping order says, 'barrels of oil.'"

"Likely story," thought LCDR Brown as he reached for the pick-axe next to the fire extinguisher, which was hanging on the bulkhead near the bottom of the ladder they had just descended.

"Keep these two covered, Cisco, while Jackson inspects one of these."

They had gone back into the middle of the barrel cargo. The XO took Jackson's carbine and trained it on the two. Commander Blair stood to one side as Jackson began to strike the top of one of the barrels. When Jackson struck the fourth time there was a gush of oil that splashed on his uniform. He pulled back. The barrel was now on its side with oil spilled all around. Suddenly, the oil stopped flowing. Something was stopping the oil from oozing out. Commander Blair yelled to Jackson to run back and get the crowbar. He handed it to the captain. Muñoz and Carlos could only look at one another. The crowbar loosened what was stopping the flow of oil. A plastic bag showed through. There it was! A clear plastic bag filled with a white powdery substance. *It had to be cocaine.* Jackson was enraged. He aimed the crowbar at Muñoz and was about to strike when the XO grabbed the tool from the sailor.

"I don't blame you for wanting to kill this guy," said the XO. "He's as much to blame for America's drug problems as anyone. We'll let the people decide his fate."

In a split second, Muñoz changed his soft-spoken tone. He began to scream out, *"¡Ahora! ¡Mátenlos!"* (Now! Kill them!)

Behind the sacks, fifty yards away at both port and starboard sides, two Colombians with bandannas around their foreheads let go with AK-47 and UZI gun fire. The boarding party on top deck, with the exception of one left to guard the twenty-three handcuffed Colombian crewmen lying face down, heard the shots and quickly scrambled down the ladder to the aid of the captain, the XO, Cisco and Jackson. It wasn't until they saw what was happening that they realized they had not handcuffed all the crew. Jackson had been hit in the left arm but was still able to aim and fire his carbine at one of the attackers. The Colombian drug runners began to yell Spanish obscenities while making their way toward the Americans. Carlos had been hit by the sub-machine gun spray and lay sprawling, blood spurting from his face and neck. Cisco, too, had been hit. He was still breathing, though laying immobile. Jackson aimed his carbine, pumped off three shots toward the advancing terrorist, and one of the bullets found its mark right between his eyes, one through his Adam's Apple and the third through the heart. Blair and XO hit the deck, pushed Muñoz down with them and covered him with their .45s. The other terrorist, seeing his companion gunned down and the additional boarding party now beginning to fire his way, was hit by six shots coming from the sailors who had just entered the area. The UZI he was carrying fell to the deck, and the machete on his side made a clanging noise against the deck as he collapsed.

Everything was deadly quiet.

Amundson, the hospital corpsman, one of the members of the boarding party, had his medical kit strapped over his shoulders, as he had been trained to do in all potentially dangerous situations. He rushed to Cisco's aid. Cisco was still alive. He had been hit just above the heart and shoulder. Jackson was quickly bandaged and resumed a ready position with his carbine. He and XO trained their weapons on Muñoz. Blair and the XO looked at Muñoz with anger in their eyes. He was immediately handcuffed. The first mate lay dead.

Muñoz looked sheepish and too scared to say anything. He knew he had used up his protective forces.

"You must have at least five tons of drugs aboard. Do you realize you're carrying millions of street dollars worth of illegal drugs? You claim to be an American citizen. Whether you knew what you were doing or not, you're a disgrace to our country, Muñoz! I hope you get what you deserve!" said the CO in a final fit of anger.

Muñoz was embarrassed.

"You're right, Captain. I should have guessed. I get paid for transporting whatever comes along. We're middlemen who simply get exports from point A to point B."

...

Later, Muñoz was to lay out his story before the Drug Enforcement Administration in Miami.

He told them that money had been the attraction for his activity in what he suspected was part of the drug trafficking game. He told them he had been involved as a skipper of these questionable vessels after he lost his family. He revealed his family and educational history. He had been appointed to the Merchant Marine Academy at Kings Point, New York, from Indiana. He had worked his way from first mate to captain of a merchant ship. His first wife, Lucille, had wanted to go back home to the Midwest to live. He tried his life as a junior executive but missed the sea. After several years he went back to driving a ship.

Lucille and the two girls, now twenty-eight and twenty-six, didn't see their husband and father very often. A divorce had ensued. When he got the job with WCI he began to make money to live and pay alimony. He was paid well and later remarried Carmen, a Cuban. He also told the Administration how happy they were living in Miami. He had never wanted to do anything wrong, he told them; he just wanted to support his lifestyle.

...

"Now we have to figure out what to do with you, your crew, and your illegal cargo," thought Phil.

As they proceeded to the main deck, Muñoz asked if the freighter was going to have to follow the submarine to a US port. Blair ignored the question. Muñoz was made to sit cross-legged with handcuffs on the top deck next to his crewmen. Both CO and XO went down the accommodation ladder and climbed into the inflatable. The wounded Jackson followed. Cisco, now showing signs of full recovery, had been taken to the sub earlier. The duty officer informed the sub's crew of the CO's approach.

Upon arriving, Captain Blair called for the communication officer and they immediately drafted a message to OP-02 breaking radio silence:

TOP SECRET
Surfaced as ordered. Intercepted, searched and arrested American skipper of *Isla Verde* under

Panamanian flag. Three Colombians killed, two *Bluefish* crewmen wounded. Ship owned by World Commerce Incorporated. Suspect cargo includes five tons drugs, marijuana and cocaine. *Bluefish.* 0800 Zulu

---

CHAPTER SEVEN

WITHIN MINUTES, Commander Blair sensed what was the only thing to do. He and LT Craemer drafted and sent the next message to Washington:

TOP SECRET
Request permission to sink *Isla Verde*. Will return US port soonest. Imperative. Deceased US sailor on board. Not casualty. Repeat, not casualty.
Advise. *Bluefish*. 0810 Zulu

Blair had recalled that this was a unique but important way to begin to dry up the supply lines of drugs infiltrating into the US. He felt it had to continue this way. The military had to step in as part of a new US policy of "no tolerance" concerning the introduction of drugs into the American nation. He would help end the scourge that was becoming, without exaggeration, as fatal as the bubonic plague that had devastated Europe.

After Washington read *Bluefish*'s messages they checked on WCI with the CIA and DEA. No question, WCI were suspected of operating out of El Salvador and Mexico. Now there was a source to tie their operation of smuggling weapons to Colombian drug traffickers in exchange for their supply. The weapons merchants, as well as other producers supplying needed products by Third World country drug lords, could begin to be tied in with new and old faces on millionaire's row in the US.

Across America, politicians, lobbyists and persons in high office had been running scared. The American people could impeach, through referendum, any public official that was slow to action. The public became convinced that it truly was "a government of, by and for the people."

They began to truly believe that they did not want to see their children die or become parasites of those who freely abused them.

...

Within hours, top level and secret meetings were called with a never-before-felt urgency. Committee members from both houses of Congress and the cabinet, along with the Joint Chiefs of Staff, met independently and then concurred by majority vote that the sinking of the disguised freighter was the only answer. The following message was sent to *Bluefish*:

TOP SECRET
Destroy freighter and cargo. Inform when accomplished. Proceed with arrested crew, St. Mary's Georgia. DEA Agents await. Plane for deceased sailor standing by.
OP-02 1800 Zulu

The Colombian crew, including Muñoz, had been herded into a *Bluefish* compartment. The dead first mate and the two dead terrorists had been placed in the reefer with EM1 Turner. Two heavily armed sailors kept close guard at each hatch. The two wounded Americans, Calderón and Jackson, were in sick bay being carefully treated.

...

Commander Blair joined the officer of the day on the bridge at the top of the sail. The submarine was directed to position itself four thousand yards away and directly perpendicular to the now-listless freighter. After watching the positioning, Blair and the OOD made their way down the ladder into the control room. The captain ordered the sub to submerge to firing depth. The sub had no sooner done that, than the CO peered through the periscope and fixed the freighter target squarely in the hair lines of the periscope sight. He gave the order to fire.

"Fire One!"

Weapons personnel fed the order into the computer. The sleek torpedoes, or "fish" as the crew called them, selected for sinking the freighter did not carry the nuclear heads but were armed with conventional warheads. Ensuring their path was the wire-guided micro chip brain.

The first weapon left the torpedo hatch. It sped silently, cutting a path through the still waters. An onlooker would have hardly detected a trace of movement as the smooth cylinder moved ahead.

Within a fraction of a second, the order from the captain was heard: "Fire Two!"

The second deadly missile was on its way.

The explosion rocked and shook the submarine. Both torpedoes had found their mark, each hitting the freighter amidships, thirty feet apart from one another. The impact split the vessel in two.

Commander Blair, spotting the direct hit, shouted, "We got 'er! It's done!" A cheer went up from the crew in each compartment. The captured crew, including Muñoz, couldn't help but know what was happening as they felt the repercussion of the explosions. Davy Jones's Locker was to be the burial ground for the poison that would have maimed thousands.

As the freighter produced one last downward pull of gushing water forming a giant whirlpool, Captain Blair composed a final message to Washington, via his senior at OP-02 in the Pentagon. The message was brief and to the point:

TOP SECRET
Mission accomplished. Five tons marijuana and cocaine
Sunk with WCI freighter. Proceeding St. Marys direct.
Bluefish. 1600 Zulu

Within minutes, an unexpected message from Washington was received by the *Bluefish* radio room.

TOP SECRET
CONGRATULATIONS. Service to the world. We salute you. The President of the United States. 2000 Zulu

The Navy's Submarine Force had begun the *real* war on drugs. Soon to follow were other elements of the Navy, Marines, Army, Air Force, and, as always, the Coast Guard. Kingpins and druglords everywhere were on notice. They would be next, no matter who they were. The American people had spoken and had persuaded Washington that "drugs are a greater threat to our national security than anything else." The preamble to the Constitution was no longer just a statement on a document written long ago. It carried the weight of all the American people.

"We the people of the United States, in order to form a more perfect Union, establish Justice, insure domestic Tranquility, provide for the common defense, promote the general Welfare, and secure the Blessings of Liberty to ourselves and our Posterity, do ordain and establish this Constitution for the United States of America."

As USS *Bluefish* (SSN-645) steamed into St. Marys, Georgia, the captain and its crew were greeted quietly by agents of the United States Drug Enforcement Administration. The freighter's skipper and his Colombian crew, still handcuffed, were put into vans and driven away. A Learjet was standing by to take Engineman First Class Otto Turner on the first leg of the trip to his resting place in Arlington National Cemetery. Captain Blair and members of the crew of *Bluefish* rendered a smart salute. Their dual mission had been accomplished.

CHAPTER EIGHT

P HIL'S THOUGHTS ABOUT THE PAST PATROL moved out of his mind. He shook his head and he realized the sedan he was in was moving away from the pier. He asked the driver to stop. He took another long look back. The Union Jack was still flying. The commissioning pennant had been taken down immediately upon his departure. The top watch was keeping a scrutinizing eye. Sunset had been at 1657 hours and the American flag rested, waiting for the new day. Thousands of United States warships commanded the seas under the Stars and Stripes. He followed the lines of the sub and saw the six-inch lines from the boat to the pier cleats. They all had just enough slack to ensure the sub's steadiness. Even at pier-side, heavy weather could cause problems. They didn't need those kind of difficulties at this point. His orders to the remaining crew before he left had been, "Be extra cautious and careful."

In a flash of introspection he asked himself, "Where will I go from here?" He knew his orders had been delayed. He didn't want to second-guess the detailer in Washington or his senior in Norfolk.

His eyes fell on the foreboding sail, dark and rising at the center, toward the heavens. The giant, wing-like planes, which controlled the ship's diving and surfacing, stood in mid-position. Together, the sail and planes resembled the tail assembly of a commercial airliner. Phil knew these essential features and the rest of *Bluefish* would never be used on patrol again. If this steel behemoth could talk it would relate some pretty hairy stories. He, as the last commanding officer, would keep their stories and many other confidential personal conflicts to himself, forever.

Just before the white sedan turned the corner of the squadron area to head toward the submarine base in Groton, where he would report to the group commander, Phil glanced amidships.

There, just behind the mid-hatch, covered by a canvas to protect against the weather, he saw one of his men enter the bowels of the whale-like ship. He thought, "Like Jonah, this man will be devoured like thousands before him, until their job is done...and then spewed out." The man saluted twice—first to the place of the national ensign and then to the top watch who represented the commanding officer. He was relieved to see the uniform of a chief with the top watch, but he still felt a strange sensation. Should he go back? He dismissed the feeling. The man going on board seemed to be in a hurry, but he had probably just forgotten something, Phil surmised. He contented himself with the fact that the man had been given permission to board. *Bluefish* was about to become history, anyway.

The skipper ordered the driver to move ahead.

CHAPTER NINE

THE CHIEF OF THE BOAT, or "COB" as he was affectionately called by the rest of the crew, was the duty chief. In a sense, he was always the duty chief. More sailors trusted him than they did the commanding officer or executive officer. He was for all practical purposes the crew's "father confessor." COB was at the quarterdeck with the top watch and made it his job to help identify each person coming or going to and from *Bluefish*.

What the CO had seen at a distance was, as he surmised, a member of the crew. COB had just appeared on top deck and recognized the sailor as he brushed past him, quickly saluting. Radioman Master Chief Daniel P. Claridge, more familiarly known as COB, a twenty-five-year veteran of the submarine service, barked and stopped the sailor in his tracks.

"Hold it, Cowboy!"

COB inspected him from head to toe. In his mind the chief thought, "Not even a first class is going to go aboard my boat on my watch without being ship-shape." COB knew that once anyone disappeared inside the steel giant that had over five million miles to its credit on nuclear power, only God knew when you'd see him again. "Cowboy" or Machinist Mate First Class Charles L. Connolly tried hard to avoid COB's questioning gaze.

"What'cha up to, Cowboy?" asked COB of the good-looking Texan dressed in his usual liberty garb—alligator-skin boots and a tall cowboy hat, today pulled down over his eyes.

"Not much. 'Scuse me, Chief, gotta get back to work," mumbled Cowboy as he almost pushed the chief aside. Without further conversation, Cowboy as much as jumped into the opening known as the midhatch. He headed down the ladder.

"Uh, oh, not a good sign," thought COB to himself. "I wonder what the hell he's doing back here so soon after leaving on liberty?" As COB looked at his watch, he estimated that Cowboy had left less than an hour ago. "A machinist mate looking for work? Oh, well, he might know something I don't." He and the top watch chuckled to themselves.

COB's attention was diverted from Cowboy by the CO's sedan, which was wending its way around the squadron headquarters building. The skipper had, only moments ago, checked out with COB and had made a remark to him that bore the mark of sadness. He had said, "Take special care of this baby, COB. We have to get it safely to another port, soon." COB had replied, "Aye, aye, sir. Have a good one."

Cowboy bounded down the ladder, two rungs at a time, and purposely missed the last four rungs. Anyone would know he was in a hurry. As he landed, he crashed into Ensign Palmer, the duty officer of the day.

Ensign Jonathan Palmer had a sense of humor. He called himself, "one lower than whale dung," a designation he perceived all officers senior to him had of lowly ensigns. He figured that if he used the insulting nickname, maybe others wouldn't, and anyway, it took the sting away, at least for a while. Lieutenant junior grade and lieutenant officers at Officer Candidate School in Newport, Rhode Island, had left no question in his mind that an ensign could be any other than the lowest form of anything. "Anyway," he thought, "laughing within himself, what better way to keep a sadistic mind quiet?" Half of the wardroom were graduates of "Canoe U," as Annapolis grads affectionately called their alma mater, the US Naval Academy. The rest of them were from a variety of NROTC University programs and Officer Candidate Schools. Thankfully, they were all pretty good guys. At times, he thought the others took advantage of the fact that he was low man in the chain of command, and to top it off, he was not yet married. He was, as a result of his single status, asked by some of the other junior officers who were married or engaged to take their duty for them. They said it would be good training and speed up his qualifications. Jonathan knew those asking him to stand their duty used that reasoning as good rationalization, but he went along with it. Being realistic, he accepted the duty for others, wanting to be a nice guy, and so he spent many hours on board. He did love to learn about all the systems on the boat, though it was painstakingly difficult to concentrate amidst the constant requirements to keep the sub in a state of readiness. Teamwork was essential. He studied hard. All systems, including the nuclear generators, which were part of the whole engineering system that made this colossus run, fascinated him.

The sudden collision with Cowboy had knocked the clip-board he was carrying out of his hand. The print-outs and schematics on the submarine inertial navigation system all went flying.

"C'mon, sailor, this isn't a flight deck!" screamed Palmer as he picked himself off the deck and gathered the scattered papers.

"Sorry, sir!" blurted out Cowboy as he hurried on without stopping to help.

By the time Palmer looked up, Cowboy was already out of sight. Palmer conjectured, "What the hell's he in a hurry about? Reckless dolt!

"Had I been a little more senior I wouldn't have hesitated to put his ass in a sling." Rodney Dangerfield's comment came to his mind: "I don't get no respect!"

By this time, Cowboy had gone down another ladder, through several hatches, and passed a number of shipmates without answering their greetings. All to a man they looked back at the rushing figure and just shrugged their shoulders. Cowboy flew through the last hatch like a bat through a dark tunnel. Ahead of him was his sleeping compartment. He knew it like the back of his hand. He parted the curtains around the front of the three-by-six-foot space he knew as his rack. Privacy was at a premium with these drawn curtains. He looked around quickly to see if anyone was looking. He heard snoring. In the far corner of the ten-man compartment he saw the reading lamp of one rack. The light was focused on a magazine. He could see a bare-breasted woman's picture on the open cover. The coast seemed clear. In what seemed an eternity, but was only a fraction of a second, Cowboy removed a small, metal object from his Levi's jacket beneath his outer, heavier leather jacket. He placed the .38 Special between the covers and thin mattress. He reached down as far as he could and placed the gun there. The man looking at the magazine with nudes stirred. Cowboy was sure he hadn't been seen.

"Gotta make a head call, dammit! Don't know why I let this happen to me. I should learn not to spend my hard-earned bread on such exciting trash, huh, Cowboy?" was Guts's embarrassed comment.

"Yeah, Guts, right on!" said Cowboy, trying to sound calm but practically choking in the process.

Guts, who had just graduated from Enlisted Submarine School at the sub base in Groton, had come to *Bluefish* just before their last patrol. It would take at least eight more months for him to qualify for the prized silver dolphins worn by enlisted men. He was hoping for another submarine out of New London. As the youngest member of the crew he took a lot of razzing, but the married guys always came around when it came time to swap duties or ask for a stand-by. He knew any exchange of money was illegal, but twenty dollars under the table seemed to be the going rate. And twenty bucks was twenty bucks. As far as he was concerned, it made the down payment on the motorcycle he was eyeing possible. As he ran into the head, he thought of the twenty he was making today and he could almost taste the feeling of power from the 1,200cc Honda he'd admired at the bike shop off Route 184 in Groton. He often dreamed of a girl sitting behind him as they sped along at 70 mph, helmets tinted, long hair flying in the breeze. Someday, the nickname Guts would be for more than his willingness to volunteer for subs at such a young age. He was ready to take a lot more risks.

Cowboy breathed a sigh of relief that Guts's quandary with his ejaculation in the head had kept him from observing him hiding the gun.

CHAPTER TEN

ENSIGN PALMER WAS NOW in the torpedo room forward of the control room. His crash with Cowboy was a thing of the past. He was now making his rounds throughout the ship and spotted Torpedoman Second Class Julian D'Cenzo off in a corner under one of the fluorescent lights. Julian was known as "Brains" by most aboard *Bluefish*. D'Cenzo liked it when an officer called him Brains. Most of them stuck to his last name, though, except Palmer. "Got the duty?" he asked of D'Cenzo.

"Nah, Mr. Palmer. Another paper due Monday. I'll be glad when I get my degree," sighed Brains.

"How much more you got before Pepperdine gives you the sheepskin, buddy?" questioned the ensign with genuine interest.

"Well, the end of the course will give me an associates degree. I really want to get a bachelor's. Think the 'Nav' will send me on to do that? I'd like to be an officer, someday. Beats this! But can't say this is a bad life. I have four more years on this tour."

"Might as well try it!" said Ensign Palmer, in an encouraging voice. "I'll help you all I can, Brains. You know that. Stick with it! The Navy's a tight little outfit and it'll do a lot for you. I bet you'll make it. Sure would like to see it happen. 'Ensign D'Cenzo' sounds pretty impressive. Bank on Navy blue—can't beat their golden opportunities," added Palmer as he playfully nudged D'Cenzo's shoulder.

D'Cenzo had been the only one in his family to be educated beyond high school. He had grown up in Chicago as a first generation Italian. That hadn't been easy. He remembered what it was like back in the ghetto of the Windy City. His father and mother still had heavy accents. They had arrived in the United States well into their teens. They had moved into an Italian neighborhood and learned English as a second language.

Michael, or Mike, D'Cenzo, Julian's father, liked to see him in uniform. The last time he was home on leave after his promotion to second class, his father had gotten very excited. Brains loved the attention he got but sometimes it was tough to handle. Like the last time, they had been gathered in the four-room apartment filled with neighborhood friends and his papa had pulled him up close. Julian's Dad was only 5'1" and he stood on his tip-toes to make himself look taller; this also helped him embrace his son. He proudly shouted over the commotion in his wonderful Italian accent, "My sohn, letsa dreenk to heem! Hees a beega man! Roonsa soobmarine, no? He shoota de feesh atta Rooshan soobs, iffa they getta too smarta." Brains had put his arm around his papa in an affectionate way, but partly to quiet him down. He remembered his mama coming to his rescue and putting her finger on her mouth, looking toward her husband, as if to say, "Shhhh." Then she motioned to everyone to sit back down and continue eating the big pasta dinner which was now in its fourth course. In his mind, D'Cenzo could savor his mama's cooking and longed for the same.

Brains had received orders to stay with the soon-to-be-decommissioned ship. Normally, it would take about a year to inactivate her. Eighty others would go with him. Many of the married men had chosen to stay in New London and catch other subs or be assigned to shore duty. In two weeks those leaving would receive permission to "leave the ship" for the last time. D'Cenzo looked forward to seeing the West Coast for the first time. He didn't want to stay in the same area for sixteen years like some he knew or heard about. "Guess if I was married or had a girlfriend it would be different," he silently pondered. "I want to get around. Washington State has a lot of rain, but at least the people are great, from what I hear!" His mind went back to his report. He knew he could finish before they left New London, and there was one good thing: no more patrols. He stopped daydreaming and got back to writing.

As Palmer left the torpedo room, he continued his brief inspection of each compartment. The duty section had to be alert. The importance of each man could not be minimized and the condition of the ship always had to be at its best. Palmer was more person- than task-oriented. He knew it wasn't always appreciated, but that's just the way he was. His mind flashed back to the last part of November when they were making their way back to the Caribbean. They had made an unscheduled stop at Roosevelt Roads Naval Station in Puerto Rico to drop off Mess Specialist Third Class Felipe Obregón. He was going to have to fly to the Philippines because of the death of his mother. The Red Cross had made all arrangements after the commanding officer had notified the man at sea. He remembered that the executive officer, Lieutenant Commander Ivan Scott, NROTC, University of Illinois, class of '76, had recommended Obregón not be permitted to go on emergency leave until *Bluefish* got to home port. The CO had overridden his recommendation and chosen to surface at Rosy Roads. As a result, Obregón was packed and on his way to McGuire Air Force Base in New Jersey, had taken a MAC flight to Travis Air Force Base near San Francisco, California, through Hawaii and was off to Manila, Philippines, long before they were scheduled to arrive in New London, Connecticut, the *Bluefish*'s home port. Palmer had a lot of respect for Commander Blair and the way he saw to it that the Navy took care of its own. He wished he could be like the CO someday.

Only ten days remained before the big sail to Washington State. Palmer knew that he was the only officer on board tonight. Only a few, like Cowboy and D'Cenzo, of the enlisted crew who didn't have duty and the duty section, were on the three hundred-foot submarine. Over one-hundred men had crossed the gangway to go on liberty at the end of the day.

Meanwhile Cowboy, by this time moving to get some chow, was in a daze. He couldn't hide his worried face. His furrowed brow, normally smooth, though a bit wind-burned, and his quiet demeanor, often boisterous, belied his efforts at nonchalance. He walked two compartments over from his sleeping quarters to the galley and the crew's mess. He liked that better than the former designation of that space as "enlisted dining facility." To a Texan, that sounded too formal. Whoever had changed it back to the more rugged-sounding term was smart. He was also glad that he didn't have to look like a junior chief when he was in uniform. Wearing "crackerjacks" was a lot better than those awful clumsy clothes that needed to be pressed and required a tie. It was much better to stuff the blues and whites in a sea-bag than carry a suitcase. "The girls," he thought, "like me in the uniform that shows off my macho figure, anyway. The chiefs can have their 'authority' clothes to wear around. Give me the salty look!" He was trying to think of everything to take his mind off the .38 Special.

Cowboy was now in the crew's mess. He poured himself a glass of bug juice. As he turned on the TV and started to watch, Brains came in for a cup of coffee. Brains scratched his head upon seeing the Texan. He was sure Cowboy had left an hour ago. Cowboy didn't make a move to greet Brains. "Strange," thought Brains..."Oh well, every man to himself." His mind wandered to the double date his buddy Tom had promised him for Saturday night. That thought quickly erased Cowboy from his mind as he sipped his cup of joe.

Torpedoman First Class Thomas G. Kozlowski had talked D'Cenzo into a blind date. He had told Brains that it would not only be great, but that he'd remember that night as long as he lived. He had wondered what that meant, but at this point he was more concerned whether his blind date would at least have a nice personality. He was sure that Tom would pick out someone who would be good to talk to and like his kind of music—a little classical with some jazz thrown in. He smelled the food cooking and he thought of what they would have tomorrow night...maybe a seven-course Italian dinner almost as good as Mama fixed. "Beer with it all will be great. I hope my date likes beer," he concluded to himself.

The evening meal was about to be served. Obregón, the duty cook who was now back from his mother's funeral in Manila, was putting the finishing touches on the night's menu. He liked to give it a home-cooked taste. There wasn't much he could do to any of it, but he added a few choice spices, oregano, bay leaf, and some garlic to the Bavarian stew. The pea soup, french fried potatoes and Jell-o were there for the taking. The coffee pot was always on. The older members of the crew downed that. The others emptied the supply of hot chocolate, milk, juice or soda without prodding. The TV was now blaring a commercial before the evening news. Cowboy couldn't stay awake. He wanted to hear if there was a change of weather. His head fell between his arms on the table.

As Palmer was finishing his rounds he stepped into the crew's mess, which was next to the wardroom, where he would eat his supper. He saw Cowboy asleep. "Strange," he thought. "First he rushes on board and practically runs me over and now he's conked out." A bit of vengeance fueled Palmer to shake Cowboy awake.

"Sailor, the rack's the place to sleep! Duty section's gotta' eat, you know!" He caught himself being angry and reverted to his usual calm mood. "Come on, Cowboy, up and at 'em. Food's on the way."

Obregón agreed within himself that the mess was no place to sleep. He didn't want to bother someone with a rank higher than he. Obregón respected higher rank, even if it was only one or two ranks above him. That's just the way it was with him. He was glad the duty officer had made it possible for him to make the mess ready for the duty section. He would not have made Cowboy move. "Sorry to bother you, Cowboy," Obregón said apologetically in his quiet tone. "Sounds like the weather's going to stay cold according to the TV."

"Aw, get off my back, dammit!" exploded Cowboy.

Palmer had gone into the wardroom, so Obregón took the brunt of his anger. He took a step back, confused. Cowboy got up, muttered obscenities and walked away. As he did, he thought, "Geez, can't get a break on this damn boat. I've gotta' figure out how I'm gonna' get out of this mess. Maybe me and this boat are coming to an end together. Damn! Damn!" He was coming back for chow soon. He definitely needed it.

CHAPTER ELEVEN

IT TURNED OUT TO BE A HAPPY COINCIDENCE that USS *Bluefish* (SSN-645) was christened and slid down the ways at the Newport News Naval Shipyard in Portsmouth, Virginia in April of 1964. At this same time, the birth of the bothered crewmember inside the twenty-five-year-old submarine was being celebrated by his parents. As Cowboy sat in the head before he went back to the crew's mess, his mind went back to his early upbringing.

Janice and Larry Connolly had always wanted the best for their second child. When he was born, that early spring in Arlington, Texas, they had felt the fresh flowers and new leaves on the trees were a harbinger of good things to come. Their newborn was unexpected. Their daughter, Susan, was already an actress on the Broadway stage. Cowboy's father had always hoped for a boy, but had given up until the surprise bundle came along. He was named Charles after his maternal grandfather and Lawrence after his father. He was the apple of their eye. Everyone agreed he was special.

Even in pre-school, and then in grade school, he constantly amazed both parents and teachers by his knowledge of boats. His interest was hard to quell. Charlie went with his dad to boat exhibits at the Dallas Coliseum. At the age of eight, while they were fishing one day, some outboard motor boats went flying by. He correctly identified their engine's horsepower and manufacturer. He talked about displacement and suggested reasons why objects heavier than water can float. Once when a sailing vessel went by, he named all of its sails without error. He knew masts from booms, mainsails from the mizzen sail and jib. He could, at ten, identify the keel, gunwale, and every part of a sailing vessel. His father beamed with pride. Charlie enjoyed the attention.

As Cowboy ran his hand through already disheveled hair and reached for the tissue, he saw himself in the mirror. He remembered the summer his parents had taken him to San Diego, California. He had devoured books about submarines before his visit. He astounded the officer on the tender who was taking them on tour. Charlie's descriptions were perfectly accurate. His interest and knowledge was rewarded by a special tour of a sub alongside the tender. The visit had stirred warm feelings for the silent service in his twelve-year-old body.

Later, a junior high school teacher confirmed that Charlie had it all together when it came to ships, and he predicted that Connolly would become one of America's fine sailors. At the age of seventeen he began to pester his parents about joining the Navy. He had finished high school early and both his parents thought this would be a good experience. They consented, having few or no reservations. His father knew his son would become a good submariner.

Now, Cowboy had been a submariner for almost eight years. On his way back to the crew's mess he filled his mind with thoughts of his early years in the Navy. He needed to get his mind off the blunder he had almost committed a few hours ago.

He wished he was back in the platoon at boot camp where he received the plaudits of his mates and the awards given to the one who was considered tops in the class. It was because of him that his platoon had also received top honors among the four platoons graduating. He wouldn't trade anything, tough as it was, for the experience at the Naval Training Center. He smiled to himself as he recalled the cheers of his platoon when he received a meritorious promotion to third class, an honor reserved for very few out of boot camp. He had also been given his choice of any "A" school. He had gone to submarine school after machinist mate "A" school at Great Lakes. It was there that his trouble began. Somehow getting beyond the nuclear power training, which followed at Orlando and Windsor Locks, was icing on the cake. The *Bluefish* assignment had come after that.

The sub school in Groton was the only one of its kind. Cowboy saw it as another boot camp. Most of his shipmates felt the same way. Just walking into the place scared you. He felt that if he could survive this, he could survive anything. The psychological testing nearly bilged him. A tendency to be claustrophobic and his young age were not helpful at the beginning. But his ability to overcome feeling trapped or closed-in disappeared, and once he settled down from being scared he seemed to mature by leaps and bounds. The academics were pretty easy, but he had to work hard to stay on top of all the assignments. He took advantage of the extra help after school hours and made sure he was tutored carefully to catch anything he missed during the trainer cycles. He wanted to be the best nuclear submariner ever.

The age of the modern nuclear submarine had come just ten years before he was born. He knew that it was his and Groton's good fortune that the first nuclear submarine, USS *Nautilus* (SSN-571), was now a part of the USS Nautilus Museum, just outside the base. His visit on several occasions had reminded him that USS *Nautilus* had accomplished many firsts, including reaching the North Pole under the cover of ice. He remembered his father's advice as he had prepared himself: "Charlie, it takes courageous men to do courageous deeds. Don't ever give up, and if you have to, take two steps back, and then move ahead again."

On his way back from the submarine school to the *Bluefish* that late afternoon, he was still stewing. "If it wasn't for all that 'Mickey Mouse' stuff they throw at you, we'd all be better submariners." He remembered saying that as a student. "Why should I call somebody 'sir' if they don't deserve it—and if we're treated like dirt? They don't deserve it," he heard himself saying. "Gold stripes don't give you the right to demand respect, just like walking into a garage doesn't make you a car." Now he was nearly twenty-five and he still held on to a deep hostility toward some of the instructors at the school. Especially one of them.

Most officers deserved to be called "sir"...but there was a chief who said he was a "chief petty officer" and insisted on being called "Sir." He acted like he was God's gift to the world. Cowboy called him a bastard under his breath. His classmates agreed.

Just as he was sauntering down the passageway to the mess, an electronics technician senior chief brushed past him. "What are you staying aboard for, tonight, Cowboy? Ain't you got anything better to do? Soup's on you know," the chief said with concern.

"Thanks, chief, sir, I'm on my way to chow. Then I plan to go back out. Probably take in a flick," answered Cowboy.

The "khaki" as chiefs were called because of their working uniform, sent his mind back into memory. The chief he had despised so much at school appeared in his thoughts.

"Thank God our guys are not like that!" he said to himself. "Here, at least, we have some say and are left alone to do our job. These guys I'll die for. Some of those in school to whom we had to cow-tow were sons-a-bitches. They deserved to die alone. I bet they could tell their grandmother to go to hell and not flinch doing it." He was glad he wasn't married to them.

His anger rose as he recalled the incident that had really ticked him off. It was during a barracks inspection. He recalled how that ogre chief who liked to be called "Sir" had made him sweep the deck of his room with a toothbrush. The only thing he'd found wrong was a piece of lint behind the radiator. The chief's stupid grin as he stood over him only made it worse. When he had finished, the straw that broke the camel's back was when the chief had said, "You're restricted from now until Tuesday morning. Report to me tomorrow, Saturday at 0730 hours." Cowboy and his buddies had planned for a three-day weekend in New York City. It had all been ruined.

Cowboy nearly tripped as he entered the crew's mess. His head had begun to clear, but not until he remembered the threat he'd made under his breath that day of the restriction: "I'll get him if it's the last thing I ever do. Not even a dog gets that kind of treatment." As a result, even today he called all chiefs "Sir." That was his way of getting back at that one chief. Others thought he was unusually polite, and they would trace it to his Texas background where children are taught to say "Ma'am" and "Sir." They would correct him, but he insisted and it grated the hell out of a few of them.

He had found that the chief he was looking for at the school had been transferred years ago. He had finally gotten up his courage to make good on his early threat. Now he wondered what he was going to do with the gun.

Cowboy sat down and immersed himself in the stew.

CHAPTER TWELVE

A MEMBER OF THE CREW who was a friend of Brains, Tom Kozlowski, pulled up in his new IROC-Z looking for a good time with Brains and some girls that night. The CO's parking spot next to the tender was vacant. He zoomed in. The squadron parking lot sentry was at the other end of the lot. What if he did get a ticket? Big deal! The *Bluefish* wasn't going to be around much more, anyway.

WQGN-FM 105.5 announced it was 5:10 p.m. and that the temperature was thirty-three degrees and getting colder. It was Saturday night. "A night for real living," thought Tom. Brains has to be finished with the report he had stayed aboard to complete. They had agreed to meet at 1700 hours. It was ten minutes past.

As he waited, he congratulated himself on the deal he had struck with Crazy Eddy, his barracks buddy, to take care of his car. Eddy Stefan had tried to get duty in Greece to visit his relatives. La Maddelena, off the coast of Sardinia, Italy, was as close as the detailer could get him. Duty aboard the Tender there counted for shore duty. He felt lucky and jumped on the chance to leave on the spur of the moment and report in early. He would take leave and do Europe later. To make things easier for himself, he had thought he would ask Tom to care for his car. It only had nine thousand miles on the odometer and he kept it spotless. Optical men were that way, spotless. Working on submarine periscopes made you that way. Those fragile and sensitive instruments required absolutely perfect conditions. Tom's only outlay would be for insurance and a very small amount each month as a gentleman's agreement for rent. "Not bad!" thought Tom. "I got a pretty good deal."

Tom could see the dark hull of *Bluefish* through the darkened surroundings of the state pier. The ship, though just under a thousand feet away, seemed farther. The blue mercury lamps overhead cast an eerie light on everything.

A big smile came over Tom's face. He let out a deafening "Yeah!" which even made the blaring six speaker Nakamichi sound system seem at mid-volume. His expression up until then had reflected his impatience. He smiled, first because he saw Brains render a "high-ball" salute, not necessarily kosher as he bounded off the sub, and second, because the night was also still young. His whole body shook with expectation.

Brains slipped on the icy concrete walk. He almost fell. It slowed him down from the loping jog with which he'd started. He caught himself as he was going down and he balanced his 180-pound body by pushing against the storage buildings that were part military, part civilian.

Merchant shipping was still a part of the old Whaling City commerce and the town fathers had shared the facilities with the Navy for many years.

When Brains got closer, Tom pressed the button that lowered his window automatically. He yelled in excited tones, "Come on, bird Brains. We've got a damn good time coming. Thought you'd never leave the nest. You've been holed in that hunk of steel long enough. Time for fun and...girls!"

"You've got it!" rejoined Brains, beginning to get caught up in Tom's excitement. His eyes widened when he saw the car. "What is this with a..." He gulped. "...an IROC-Z? Awesome! Where'd you get that? My favorite color, too!" It was bright, waxed and without a blemish; cranberry red. Brains let out a yell that could be heard back on the tender, "Whoopie! God A'mighty!"

Tom revved up the 350-horsepower engine. The twin exhausts popped as he burnt rubber backing up. He rounded the corner from pier site, the radio blasting in all directions.

The sentry on the tender, Roberts, tried to catch the license number on the car. The chief of the watch joining him in the glassed-in enclosure grabbed the binoculars to help spot the speedster to no avail. All they were able to see was the red shape going off into the night with headlights burning.

"Just a kid. Probably an officer's dependent," commented the older sailor. "Whoever it is'll surely get plastered against a concrete column of an over-pass or'll go across the median and kill some innocent passengers. It's a bad night for speeding. Pretty slick out!"

The seaman who had sentry duty agreed, but secretly wished he would be lucky enough someday to own a sweet buggy like that.

Tom and Brains were now heading for Groton at break-neck speed. The hard rock music from the radio was interspersed with commercials and "jokes" from the DJ.

"Why did the chicken cross the road?" asked the DJ.

A wimpy, high-pitched voice answered, "I guess to get to the other side!"

"Oh, you dumb nut," said the DJ. "Wrong again. It got smashed by a passing Porsche, never did make it to the other side. The chicken had a death wish, 'bone' and all!"

Canned laughter and hoots and whistles filled the car from the speakers. Tom and Brains howled!

As far as Tom was concerned, he was having fun driving "his" new car. He wasn't the least bit interested in observing the safety measures the law had provided. He ignored stop signs; honked under overpasses; turned right at the red light without stopping first and accessed Federal Highway 95 at top speed, the tires of the IROC-Z squealing all the time. What Tom had forgotten was that Highway 95 was carefully patrolled by marked and unmarked police cars. Tom knew that it was a major highway running all the way from the Canadian border to Miami, Florida. In fact, when Tom was younger, he and his folks had vacationed 150 miles south of Miami at the Southernmost Point Motel in Key West. Tonight, he felt like he owned the road, any road.

As they began to cross the Gold Star Memorial Bridge's span heading north toward Providence and Boston, they failed to see a Connecticut

State Police car at an emergency turn-around access and popular hiding place, with overgrown bushes now filled with ice crystals, for police to deter speeders. Tom had just pressed the "pedal to the metal" and had been doing over 85 mph. He had slowed down to seventy-five at Brain's insistence. Suddenly, at mid-bridge as they approached the New London/Groton city line, the police cruiser let go with its sirens and flashing lights. The spotlight was turned on and shone squarely on the driver.

Tom raised his hands to his head in desperation. He practically pulled his hair out. He couldn't believe his bad luck. His knees felt weak. His stomach churned. If he'd had some toilet tissue, he could have used it. Brains, too, put his head between his hands and started to shake.

Tom pulled the car over.

"Oh, God, Tom, we shouldn't have started out so damn fast! Geez, we'll be late for our date!"

"Don't get me more nervous, just shut up! Be grateful I have my license and registration. Here comes the stupid cop. Don't say a word," Tom advised.

They rushed to buckle themselves but the policeman got to the window, which Tom opened, before they could adjust the seat belts.

"What do you have against the state emission law?" the lawman asked.

Tom wasn't prepared for that question. He saw that the emission sticker was a month past due, and remembered that Eddy had told him to get it updated. The cop continued his questioning as Tom handed him his license and registration.

"Don't like to buckle up, huh? I've never unbuckled a dead person, as the saying goes. Guess you're in the business of angel manufacturing," the cop added cynically. "What do you think this is, the Indianapolis Motor Speedway? How fast would you guess you were going? By the way, turn down that damn radio, NOW!"

In the excitement, Tom and Brains had forgotten to lower the volume. The station had been playing Van Halen's "Eruption." The cop pulled out his book of tickets and started to write. Tom handed him his Navy identification, hoping to get away with just a warning.

"Oh, my God, not Navy guys! I really hate to pinch old buddies," he remarked somewhat sarcastically. "Submariners, no less. That's even worse!"

Tom wasn't sure whether to breathe more easily. He knew they'd been had after the next verbal onslaught by the policeman. The cop adjusted his chinstrap, part of the police winter uniform.

"Now, I was with the *real* Navy," said the cop. "*Surface!* Destroyers, in my day. That's the only way."

The temperature of both submariners rose.

The cop went on, "Damn Bubbleheads. Bunch 'a patsies, hiding underwater. Well, you weren't four hundred feet under tonight, and I've got you good!"

With each comment the two sailors were becoming more livid. They felt like laying into him and his monkey suit, but they saw the gun in his holster which was unsnapped, just in case. They also saw the fire in his eyes. Tom thought, "Maybe I'll burn rubber and leave this asshole in the dust. No, he can call another cop on his radio or he'll shoot one of our tires out and then where'll we be?" He decided to cool it. The policeman went on.

"When did you get this car?"

"Just today. Well, it actually belongs to a buddy as you see by the registration. He's off to the Med. I'm taking care of it while he's gone.

This is the owner's letter giving me permission to use and take care of his car in his absence."

The policeman looked at the papers and gave them back to Tom. He seemed satisfied. In a final effort to win the cop's sympathy, Tom said, "Brains, here, and I are on our way to pick up a couple of hot dates. I'll be more careful, sir, honest!"

"So, a piece of ass is more important than obeying the law, huh?" muttered the cop, hoping not to be heard.

Brains thought, "What a gross remark! Uncalled for!"

"You damn well better slow down," said the cop. "I honestly don't care what happens to you, but there are a lot of innocent people out there whose lives *do* matter. I should have you follow me to the station and impound this death trap, but I'm giving you a ticket instead."

Tom looked at the ticket as the officer walked back to his police cruiser. "Christ! $250 bucks!" The itemized violations included: "failure to have an up-to-date emissions sticker"—$50; "no seat belt"—$50; "Exceeding the 55 mph speed limit"—$50; plus $5 for every mile over 55 mph—$100. The cop pulled by in his cruiser as Tom said, "This dude must think I'm Donald Trump. Hey, Brains, you've got half a share in this, okay?"

That comment hit Brains like a ton of bricks. He'd been saving his money for college. Not knowing how else to reply, he said, "Yeah, sure, Tom, whatever you say."

"All right!" agreed Tom gustily. That calmed him down.

They proceeded at the marked speed limits, turned off on the first exit and Tom spotted a gas station. "Gotta' take a leak. Fill 'er up while I go." The gas tank was nearly empty. Tom got the restroom key from the young attendant who was staring at the shiny IROC-Z glowing in the neon-lighted pump area.

A moment of panic ran through Brains. He felt shivers up and down his spine. He thought about his blind date. "What if she's a pig? She may be terrible!" Every negative possibility rushed through his already frazzled mind. The station attendant took twenty-five dollars for the gas. Brains was already $150 into it and the night hadn't even started. Tom slid back in behind the wheel and didn't even bother to ask the price of the gas or if he could share the cost. Brains said nothing.

They sped toward the rendezvous point. In less than a minute they were on Long Hill Road. The plan had been to pick up the girls, eat, and fly back to the New London/Waterford side, across the Thames River to Cinema 8. They were already fifteen minutes late. Tom and Brains spotted the girls huddled up in the shadow of the mini-mall buildings. Tom recognized his date. He had been with her before. Brains's blind date was someone Tom hadn't laid eyes on.

CHAPTER THIRTEEN

ROSIE WAS OLDER than Brains expected. Her mod clothes and heavy mascara made her look younger. Her long brunette tresses were hidden by the upturned collar of the pad-lines corduroy jacket around which she wore a long angora plaid scarf. The car came to a screeching halt to avoid running her down. She had caught a glimpse of Tom and waved frantically, not watching where she was stepping.

"Hi, Honey!" she called, not caring about the near miss.

"Damn, what'e hell ya' doin'?" Tom was still burning from the traffic tickets. Brains couldn't believe this was the same Tom he knew.

Tom was wearing jeans, loafers, and a smart-looking designer polo shirt. A fur-collared Naval Air Force pilot's jacket in dark brown leather covered his torso. He had picked it up at the Army-Navy store in Newport, Rhode Island. He was wearing shades, $110 gargoyles, "44 Blues," and had just put them on the dashboard. That outfit made him even more popular with the girls. Brains got out of the front seat and Rosie settled into the bucket seat, getting as close to Tom as she could. She immediately put her hand on his leg, gave him a long kiss and asked, "What made you late?" She caressed Tom's face and looked at him with longing eyes.

Brains and his blind date stood outside the car. He wasn't quite sure how to proceed.

"Come on, Brains, get in!" yelled Tom.

Brains pushed the front seat forward, excused himself for possibly crushing Rosie, and politely invited his date to get in. She slid across the back seat and Brains tumbled in beside her. He let the front seat slam back into place. As he tried to close the door, he thought his arm would break. Tom and Rosie were oblivious to everything as they clung madly to each other. Tom was not about to lose the chance to start his romancing. In the back by now, they looked at each other in embarrassment, a nervous smile on both their faces. They hadn't been introduced. Brains was about to break the silence when Rosie stopped in mid-kiss from Tom and turned around.

"Oh...sorry!...Tommy, darlin', let's not be so rude to our friends. Introduce me to your good-lookin' friend."

Tom screwed up his face and made an indecent gesture behind Rosie's back.

Rosie added, "Gotta' get these kids to stop guessing who each other's with." She smiled and snuck a wink at Brains.

"Rosie, this is Brains," said Tom. "He's one of the smartest guys in the world. If you don't believe it, ask him. I'd like to think he's shy, but probably just slow to the draw, know what I mean?" A devilish laugh surrounded his next words, "We're going to fix that!"

D'Cenzo wasn't sure what that meant.

Brains's date was dressed in loose black slacks, a yellow turtleneck sweater covered by a red three-quarter length coat. She pulled the coat belt around her even tighter. The temperature had dropped to two degrees and even in the car her teeth were chattering. The IROC-Z's heater was working hard to warm things up.

Rosie said, "Tommy, meet my friend, Candy. Candy, meet Brains." She looked at Brains and asked, "Is that your real name?"

D'Cenzo felt squeamish...

"Real name's Julian...Julian D'Cenzo," he said.

Candy, acting coy, said, "Pleased to meet you."

Rosie didn't skip a beat, and interrupted: "Hi, Brains, I like that nickname. Cute! I love people with smarts." She winked at D'Cenzo. "We'll have to get together, sometime."

Tom slapped Rosie's leg.

"Get offa' that goop," he said. "You're my date, remember?"

Rosie sank back into the seat as though hurt.

Candy giggled. Beneath the coat were a few hidden pounds. She was definitely overweight. Candy had a smooth face, almost porcelain-looking from the cleansing cream she used twice a day. Selling Mary Kay part time, after her main job at the Salvation Army used clothing store in New London, wasn't very profitable, but it provided her with expensive facial and bodily preparations. Candy's flowing blond hair was a definite asset. She gave her head a quick flick to get her hair away from her eyes and it partially fell on Brains's lap. He liked that! It felt soft, as did her hand when she reached over. Brains wasn't sure what that lump in his throat was about.

"Okay if I call you Julian? I really like that. Makes me think of warm weather in July. Glad the heater's working. Brrrr! I'm cold!" Secretly she wished Julian would cuddle up, but he kept his distance. "This is an awesome car," she rambled on. "Where you from? You're real nice-lookin'. Been lookin' forward to tonight. Where we goin' to eat?"

Brains thought she'd never stop. Food was definitely on her mind. "This is going to be an expensive evening, I can see that," he thought.

Tom floored the IROC-Z and Brains kept his distance from Candy as they all began to search out a good place to eat among the variety of restaurants, mostly fast food, along Long Hill Road.

Brains, who was also wearing jeans, had a collegiate look, unlike his leather-jacketed buddy. His gray pullover covered a cream-colored shirt. He had purchased them for this occasion. A light blue quilted jacket and rabbit-fur-lined gloves completed his wardrobe.

Candy continued her incessant jabbering. "Where ya' from? I bet your family's rich and famous. I can tell by the way you're dressed." She covered her mouth each time she smiled to hide a missing tooth. And almost every time she spoke, she followed with a giggle, so her hand was often up to her mouth. "Hey, Rosie, don't you think Julian here looks right out of a movie? I bet your folks live in Beverly Hills."

Rosie was too busy looking out the window. The question slipped by. "My daddy's in North Dakota now," said Candy. "Family lived all over, though. My daddy was in the Army in Hawaii when I was born. Momma died some years ago. Daddy always wanted to farm, so when he left the Army that's what he did. Many's the night he'd tell us he couldn't wait to get back on the farm so's he could enjoy life without constantly being told what to do. You know how the Army is..." She chuckled all by herself.

Rosie gave her a side glance, one eyebrow raised. "Ooh, sorry my li'l SUBmariner," she said. She pronounced it wrong and that grated Tom's ears.

"It's subMARINEer," he shouted back.

She retreated.

Brains couldn't answer any of Candy's questions. She wouldn't let him get a word in edgewise. She'd probably forgotten she wanted to know where he was from, anyway. He too, was ready to eat, but not for the same reason as his date. He was sure, looking at her, she just wanted to stuff herself.

He looked at his watch and said, "Hey guys, if we're going to make that 7:15 flick we'd better get something in fast foods. There's a Pizza Hut down the block." Italian food of any kind was better than anything else so far as he was concerned. Agreement was reached with no hassle and Tom screeched to a fast stop, turned in to a Pizza Hut and made a fast right into a parking spot. The four rushed out of the car and the cold air into the Hut.

They placed an order. Brains thought Candy would never stop asking for what she wanted. Rosie, Tom, and Brains ordered a small combination pizza and a medium drink. Candy added a salad, a large chocolate milkshake, and a large order of fried onion rings. She also asked for an order of garlic bread while she waited for the pizza. Brains wanted to nudge Tom, to ask, "What did you get me into?" But Tom and Rosie were already on their way to a booth, arm in arm. Brains thought, "What a bust!"

Rosie and Tom seemed oblivious to everything. Now and then Rosie would take her eyes off Tom long enough to eat. Once she said, "Candy, get a little closer to Brains. He looks lonesome. If I were you, I wouldn't let that handsome hunk even an inch away. He doesn't bite... or do you, Brains?"

Candy giggled, made a motion in Brains's direction, and then dipped into her plate. She cleaned it and then reached over for Brains's leftovers.

"Hope you don't mind, Julian," she said.

He liked being called Julian. His mother called him that, except she made it special: "mi Julio," she would say. And the other difference was that Candy's voice sounded hollow.

Candy finished up everyone's leftovers. Brains looked at his watch and announced they had better get going. They wildly ran across the parking lot to the red IROC-Z, careful not to slide on the rock-salt-sprinkled area. Candy stuffed her mouth with one last piece of Tom's cheese pizza as she wrapped a muffler over her ears.

Tom was careful going back on the southern span of the Gold Star Memorial Bridge, named in honor of Connecticut's WWII dead. They took off at Crossroads exit, drove a little ways on Parkway South and turned into the new Caldor Mall, which also contained the Waterford Cinema 8 theater. The large parking lot was more crowded than usual. Customers were accommodated inside to get tickets because of the cold. Brains got some money from Tom and stood in line for the tickets while Tom and the girls stood in line at the concession stand. Tom ordered a bucket of popcorn for each twosome. Candy made sure theirs had a lot of butter.

As they waited for the movie to start, Brains looked at Tom and Rosie. They were already in a mad embrace.

Five minutes into the movie, Candy asked if Brains could go out and get her another bucket of popcorn. She had practically finished the first all by herself. Brains excused himself as he tried to squeeze out of the row. As he returned, he brushed up against the knees of a woman sitting in the second seat of his row, lost his balance, and dropped some of the popcorn on her lap. She let out a scream, causing Tom to say, loudly, "You crazy, oaf, Brains. Sit down!" Brains scrunched down near Candy, handing her the popcorn, which he hoped would keep her from her constant chatter. Brains tried to enjoy the movie through the munching of un-popped popcorn. Candy was savoring each bite. He tried to pretend she wasn't there. He sat back and enjoyed the film, a replay, it seemed, of his own family in Chicago, about an Italian community. The movie alone had made the night worthwhile.

On the way home, Tom asked, "Hey, Brains, want t' spend the night at Rosie's? Candy lives there, too, ye' know."

He hadn't known that they lived together.

"Well..." he hesitated. "If you don't mind taking me back to the sub, I'd prefer..."

"Oh, come on!" insisted Tom. "Stay the night. I'll drive you back early."

"But I've got duty. You know how hard it is to get up. I really should go back now." Brains wasn't looking forward to spending more time with Candy.

"I promise to get you back in time! Trust me!" Tom appealed.

The sub was being left farther behind as they traveled back into Groton. Both girls exchanged a look of approval exchanged.

It was nearly 11:00 p.m. when they got back to the apartment. Rosie pulled out some glasses from a cabinet above the kitchen sink and a couple of fifths of rum and vodka. The mixes, Coca-Cola and 7Up, were in the fridge. Candy, who wasn't twenty-one yet, sipped the drink Tom had fixed for her. Brains had refused to have any, offering his going on duty the next day as an excuse. After his first mixed drink, both Tom and Rosie had a beer. Tom had stopped at Hodges Square and picked up three six-packs. He had brought them when they were going back to Groton from the movie in Waterford. Now, Brains knew Tom and Rosie had planned all this. Some buddy!

After Tom's heavy drinking, including two beers and his third mixed drink, several hours had passed. Tom's voice sounded clipped. The television had been showing an X-rated HBO film.

Tom was using profanity every third word. He was practically slobbering over Rosie, who was getting pretty drunk, too. She became annoyed at Tom's advances in front of Candy and Brains. Tom said, "Gott'a let Brainsh know what lifsh all 'bout, love," slurring his words. Candy was dipping into the peanuts. She had left her mixed drink and was now drinking beer. She insisted she was hungry, opened the refrigerator and pulled out a dish of pudding. Then she fixed herself a dish of peanut butter ice-cream, took some Oreo cookies and sat in front of the TV. She paid no attention to Brains. He sat in a recliner and began to fall asleep.

Rosie and Tom, who had been making love in another corner of the living room, looked up, saw the other two doing their own thing and quietly slipped into one of the bedrooms. Rosie was almost undressed with Tom having been all over her. She went into the bathroom while Tom finished undressing. He had slipped between the sheets.

...

It was now nearly 4:00 a.m. Brains was heading in the direction of USS *Bluefish*. He was petrified. His mind was racing. He had left Candy with a stranger, who had kicked him out of the apartment and thrown the keys to the IROC-Z at him. The stranger had told him to be sure and open the trunk, later.

CHAPTER FOURTEEN

IT WAS SUNDAY, Brains's duty day. He had arrived on *Bluefish* just two hours before going on watch, at 0545. He had been too scared to open the trunk of the car before he parked, but once there, he gingerly pulled the trunk door up. Shivers went up and down his already cold body. He had driven in the dark, but remembered bloodstains as he left the apartment in the dark. Now, as he opened the trunk, Tom's nearly frozen body, with blood still partially pooling, and a strong smell of alcohol caused Brains to partially throw-up and gasp in unbelief. He quickly closed the trunk. He ran to the sub, quickly moved past the Watch, slid down the ladder and made his way to his sleeping compartment. Sliding beneath sheets and a blanket on his rack, he tried, without success, to catch an hour of sleep and mustered with the duty section and the duty officer at 0745 in the control room. He held his breath, hoping that no one else knew what had happened.

After standing his watch, which was from 0800 to 1200, he tried to go to sleep. He tossed and turned in the rack, which was the third of three in the tier. He could only think, "If only I was at sea, I would be in a haven away from all this." His anxiety kept him from eating breakfast and lunch. He was sure nothing would stay down. He tried reading. No luck! His mind was a-whirl. He'd have to go back on the midnight watch. He had to figure out what to do, as Tom's body in the trunk kept appearing in his mind.

...

Suddenly, as he was about to go to sleep, the sub's warning alarm sounded. Someone had broken into an unauthorized space. Brains ran through the passageway, hatch through hatch and up a ladder. It was 1423. He was in officers' country. The officer of the day and chief of the watch were grilling three frightened teenage boys. Their hands were in the air and they were lined up against the passageway bulkhead.

Commander Blair's oldest son, Jim, had just gotten his license. He had looked forward to his sixteenth birthday for that reason alone. Estelle, Phil's wife, couldn't explain to Phil what she felt were real serious problems with Jim. As far as Phil was concerned, his son could do no wrong. But Jim and his two friends, now lined up as common criminals in *Bluefish*, had some of their own explaining to do.

Last Friday, Jim had argued with his dad that he would not go to New York to watch a play. He had invited his friends, Butch and Goose, to visit the submarine. He thought this would please his father, but what he really wanted to do was to show them how he could drive. He knew the way to *Bluefish* because he went with his dad so often. A solution was finally reached when Phil said they could visit on Sunday, if Jim went to the play. He couldn't understand why Jim had chosen these friends. At Ledyard High School, Jim had befriended these two unlikely candidates. He knew they had problems. Something inside of him made him feel there was a way of helping them. He was criticized for not choosing better friends.

Butch was an acne-covered and overweight fifteen-year-old. His real name was George Frompier and his parents had settled here from Canada. When Butch was in the third grade, his mother and father had separated and eventually divorced. As a result, his mother worked full-time and let him and his younger twin brothers fend for themselves. Butch had been caught shoplifting at Stop & Shop and Caldors in Groton, but had been treated as a juvenile, and the judge had placed him in the custody of his mother, Claire, with a warning. He continued to shoplift without being caught. He would turn what he had into cash and buy what he wanted. He was always one step away from the police.

The other member of the triumvirate was Goose, age sixteen. He was the opposite in physical appearance from Butch. Goose was gangly, almost six feet, two inches, and wore a punk rock haircut that made him look even taller. The sides of the haircut were dyed blonde and the top was his natural light brown. His father, a welder at the Electric Boat plant, which was now manufacturing the 688 class submarines and Trident 727 class subs for General Dynamics Corporation and the US Government, had joined the Metal Workers Council strike for higher wages and more increased benefits. Management had told them their contracts were slowing down and they couldn't do anything for them. They were also told that the Trident program, one of the top elements in the Triad in the Defense Department, was being reviewed. They were investigating smaller and faster subs for the future. There would no be raises until the Pentagon agreed to their strategy for building. The union insisted that regardless of the contracts, their people needed to be properly remunerated. Inflation did not permit their workers to afford the cost of living under the present wage system. Goose's father, Pierre, was hoping the strike would end soon. Pumping gas and washing cars did not provide the support the family needed, even if his wife, Dolores, was clerking at the nearby Crystal Mall in Waterford. Neither Pierre nor Dolores could be counted on to be home when Goose and his sisters, Nancy and Brigette, arrived from school. Goose called his sisters a "pain in the ass" to their faces and to anyone who would listen. There wasn't much love lost between them.

Butch and Goose had started out together in school. They made quite a pair, one tall and skinny, the other fat and pimply. Kids at school laughed behind their backs and called them "Laurel and Hardy." When Jim came along two years ago, he had met them in middle school and then gone on to high school with them. There was hardly a time they were not together. Jim gave them some respectability. Even though others felt he was hurting himself by having these friends, he had unselfish motives to help them. He'd always been for the underdog. His approach was to "walk the talk."

Jim had invited his friends to visit *Bluefish*. He thought this would help them see a side of life that would change their perspective. The top watch recognized Blair's son and admitted all three. Butch and Goose showed their school IDs and Jim vouched for them. Because Jim was the CO's son and dependent, no escort was provided.

"Come on guys, this is the chance of a lifetime," Jim told his two friends. "Not many people get to see a real submarine, especially one in an operational squadron. My old man says this one's about to be inactivated but it's still in A-1, ready-for-war condition."

The Duty Section was watching *Beverly Hills Cop* in the crew's mess. Popcorn, ice-cream and the machines with the bug juice were available. The sailors were cheering for Eddie Murphy, and deeply engrossed in the flick. Thinking they would get more out of their visit by seeing the spaces, Jim motioned to his friends to follow him. Since Eddie Murphy had the crew in stitches, they paid no attention to the three adolescents who slipped right by them.

Normally, Officers' Country was out of bounds to everyone except officers. An exception was when the crewmember or visitor was on official business. The fact that Jim was the CO's son, was recognized, and had been aboard many times before, made it easy for him, Butch, and Goose to roam that area of the sub freely. Enlisted men stayed away from Officers' Country. Sub crews tended to be a lot closer with less class distinction than at shore stations or on large Navy vessels, but the difference remained. Sailors preferred not to mix with officers.

The three walked into the empty wardroom. Jim sat at the head of the conference/dining table. The similarity in looks between Commander Blair and his son were striking. A no-nonsense person, the CO had the respect of all the crew. His two years as the skipper had been unusually devoid of anything but positive handling of all situations. Jim assumed a stern, yet friendly appearance, to imitate his father. Butch and Goose sat on either side. They all scanned the room in which the officers of *Bluefish* conducted their business, watched movies and work connected videos, and ate their meals.

It was hard for them to imagine that as many as twelve full-size men could fit into this seemingly small space. There was no space to spare. An overhead screen was rolled up into its metal case above one end of the table. Projectors were stored in cabinets across and above the table. Books, mostly professional and schematics on *Bluefish*'s nuclear reactor and engineering system, submarine inertial navigation system, the weapons system, the ship's inter-communication and others lined the shelves. The volumes of *Jane's Fighting Ships* and one book on Russian and other foreign vessels were part of their library. The ship's crew had only seen the Russian subs and surface vessels as light blips by radar through periscope sighting at safe and undetectable distances. The wardroom was on the first level below the top deck. Three levels, including the bilges, were below.

Thoughts of his father came to Jim as he sat there. He knew that his dad went on patrol, sometimes for twelve or more weeks at a time. They could spend sixty or more days under the surface of the sea. Nuclear power, he was told, could provide an almost unending source of power. His father, as all submariners were, was sworn to secrecy. They never spoke about their patrols. Not even his mom or any wife or girlfriend was privy to what went on. For fun, Jim pretended he was in the control room and acting like a commanding officer.

"Up periscope!" he told his school chums.

Butch, very much into it, correctly responded, "Up periscope, aye, sir!"

"Land ho!" interjected Goose.

They all burst out laughing.

Their game didn't last long. To avoid boredom, Jim said, "Let's look around." They stepped out of the wardroom to the captain's stateroom, with which Jim was familiar. He had been there numerous times. He knew it was probably locked but he tried the handle anyway. It moved!

He motioned to the others to follow him in. They resembled the Three Stooges on tiptoes as they walked in.

Butch and Goose had never been on a submarine. They looked carefully. Everything was smaller than normal. "Spartan" was the word for the small room's appointments. The aluminum basin in the officers' staterooms matched the aluminum medicine cabinet above it. The three saw their reflections as they moved toward the single bed, tightly made up. The officers' beds were made up by men from the supply department, usually those who were assigned mess duty. They were supervised by the mess specialists.

Butch stopped in front of the mirror and saluted himself in British fashion, stuck out his chest, only to realize that his belly was still hanging over his tightly drawn belt. In a squeaky voice, more so than his normal tone, he said, "I am the captain. Do as I say!"

Jim and Goose stood in mock attention, then stuck their tongues out as if on cue. Goose added to his antics, "Make us, fat one! Maybe if we have a smoke, we'll feel like taking your orders, oh doughnut shape!"

Butch flinched at the name-calling, but when smoking was mentioned he forgot the hurt. He had brought his supply of marijuana just in case. They all quickly sat on the edge of the captain's rack, an all-metal piece of furniture, a bit wider than the enlisted racks. Most everything on a submarine is metal, except the fire-proof synthetic plyboard used for bulkheads, ceilings, and cabinets.

Jim was about to squelch the smoking idea but Goose pleaded, "Just a couple of drags, Jimbo, please!"

Though he was scared, Jim consented, but he added, "If we're found out, Dad'll never forget it!"

"Oh," said Butch, "fat chance!"

Butch pulled out a small bag containing the marijuana and cigarette paper. He rolled his own quickly, pinching each side to contain the seeds, bits of leaves, and twigs. Then he lifted the limp cigarette to his mouth and Goose lit it for him with a stick match he'd taken out. The flame almost singed Butch's eyelashes.

"You dumb nut!" cried Butch.

Goose stepped back nervously, but didn't apologize. He wanted a drag, too, and said, "Come on man, don't hog that reefer all to yourself!"

Jim hadn't noticed that after lighting the stick, Goose had thrown the lit match into the small trash container next to the desk. On the desk were Commander Blair's neatly stacked notebooks and papers.

In jest, Jim said, "If you don't let Goose have a smoke, I'll call the OOD."

At that time, he suddenly heard the alarm, which he assumed was a drill. He did not suspect that the alarm had been set off by the heat of the fire that had started in the wastebasket where the match had landed. The sensors for fire on the submarine were extremely sensitive. Submariners feared any fire on their boats, nuclear or not. It was more feared than ocean water from a burst pipe or a hole in the hull caused by crashing into another vessel, rock formations or other objects. Everyone was trained to retain the flood which might occur with bulkhead damage, but FIRE put fear into everyone. Jim's jesting remark about the officer of the day was about to become a reality.

...

"Fire!" called the fire watch, a seaman from the "A" Gang.

"Fire in Officers' Country!" yelled the duty chief.

"Fire!" boomed out the duty officer over the 1MC. He bounded down the ladder from the quarterdeck where he's been checking the log. "All hands report to watch stations. First Section report immediately to Officers' Country."

...

It didn't take long for the fire to catch the attention of the teenagers. Jim suddenly realized that the alarm was caused by the smoke which they all saw. The trash had not been emptied and the flames had licked the side of the desk.

"Oh, God," Jim sputtered. "Oh, my God, now I've done it!"

His hands were wet with perspiration. He hit his hand on the desk in an angry gesture, and at the same time he tried to smother the flames with the pillow Goose had thrown at him. Butch and Goose then stood petrified.

Jim yelled, "Put the damn weed down the basin!"

Between Butch and Goose trying to wash the marijuana down and Jim trying to put out the fire, they got in each other's way. It was all a huge confusion.

The officer of the day, or duty officer, rushed in. A fire watch followed carrying a fire extinguisher. He turned it upside down, released its chemicals and soon had the fire under control. Jim and his two friends had scrambled against the rack, scared to death. The OOD stared at them in disbelief. "What the hell do you think you're doing? Who let you come aboard?" He looked at Jim, recognized him as the skipper's son and asked him, point-blank, "Who are these guys?" Their appearance made them questionable characters. The OOD looked at the basin. The water was still running. The soot marks of the cigarette were still visible. "What is that in the basin?" he questioned. The three gave no answer.

The OOD ordered the chief of the watch to arrest the three. They ordered the three to step out into the passageway, face the bulkhead with their hands above their heads, legs spread apart and they were searched for weapons or other contraband. The bag of pot was taken from Butch and the matches from Goose.

"We were only visiting my father's stateroom," apologized Jim to the OOD, as tears welled up in his eyes. "These are my friends from school."

"I'm sorry," Butch, the youngest of the three, cried as he lost control of himself. He blubbered, "Oh, God, oh, Jesus, what have I done? I... I...I...it was all my fault."

Goose was too scared to say anything. He felt sick.

They were all escorted into the wardroom and questioned further. Jim's ID card confirmed that he was the son of Commander Phillip

E. Blair, *Bluefish*'s commanding officer. A telephone call had also confirmed it. The CO informed the OOD that he'd be right over.

Butch and Goose sat quietly across from Jim. They looked down and then looked up to glance at one another only once as they listened to the OOD's lecture. He told them about the dangers of drugs, and about the danger of being in unauthorized spaces. He specifically lectured them about the Submarine Force's absolute zero tolerance of drug use and abuse. As he continued to chew them out with caustic words, the chief of the watch was finishing up the incident report. Just then, *Bluefish*'s skipper walked in.

Jim wished he could just disappear. He saw the look of utter disappointment and disgust on his father's face. The nervous smiles, which the three had managed a few seconds earlier, were now totally wiped away. The OOD finished briefing the CO and, at his request, was given the three in custody. As they walked off the gangway into the afternoon, it seemed more bleak and cloudy and cold for Jim, than it really was.

Goose had let Jim drive his car since Jim had just gotten his license. As he and Butch sat there, Commander Blair said harshly to them through the open window, "I don't ever want to see you with my son again, hear me?" As he and Jim got into their car, he simply said to his son, "How could you do this to me? My own ship! My own state room. You've disgraced me in front of my crew!" Jim wanted hard to say something. He choked back tears. He knew that to say he was sorry would only further enrage his dad. He wished he could crawl into a hole and die. You could hear a pin drop the rest of the ride home to Ledyard.

CHAPTER FIFTEEN

BRAINS RETURNED TO THE WEAPONS SPACE among the torpedoes. On watch and off, he had been wondering what to do about Tom's body in the trunk of the IROC-Z.

"I've got to get off this boat," he thought to himself. An answer came to him. He could get permission to go to the squadron recreation center above the parking lot. He had begun to devise a plan to somehow hide the body that had now been inside the car for nearly twelve hours. He hoped rigor mortis had not set in. He really wished that Tom was still alive. Every possible solution had been considered. The most obvious one was to report the death to the authorities and let the investigation begin. He was too scared to try that route, though it made the most sense. He just didn't want to be implicated at a time when so much was going his way: getting his degree, going to the state of Washington, and having the support of both officers and his sailor buddies as he sought a commission. If he got involved in a murder investigation, the crew would always hold it against him. He knew he wasn't guilty, but everyone would wonder. He would go back on watch in four hours. It was 1600.

Daylight would last for another sixty minutes. He had to work fast. He had received permission to leave the boat from the section leader. He headed toward the recreation center and just before he got there he looked around, saw no one near, and headed toward the car. As he did so, he was still considering the many possibilities for hiding Tom's body. He thought, "I can put it in a dumpster, or toss it in the Thames River, or drag it to the empty fields near Parkway South and bury it. No! Maybe, just maybe, the best thing to do would be just to leave Stefan's car parked where it is. Eventually it would be picked up as a deserted vehicle or an obstruction to snow removal. The police would immediately look to the owner as the prime suspect. And Eddy Stefan's in La Maddelena."

...

A brilliant idea came to his mind.

His courses in criminology with Pepperdine had suggested that no one had ever committed the perfect crime. This fascinated him. Why not him? He could go down in history! For a moment a veil of guilt enveloped him. But that guilty feeling didn't last long. He relished the idea of participating in the perfect crime. He wished it hadn't fallen on him to try to hide the body. He wasn't sure at all why he was involving himself in this way. He vacillated. His desire to make history drove him to finish out the risky job he'd set out to do. He ran to the diving barge which was somewhat removed from the tender. He hoped that his friend, Hull Technician Second Class Robert W. Finney, would be there.

A familiar voice greeted him. "Hi, Brains! How's the world treating you? Man, you look frozen. Come on in and have some joe. Sit down!" Bob warmed up the brew and sat on the edge of the duty bunk.

"Thank God you're here!" exclaimed Brains, still breathing heavily from the block-long run. He rubbed his cold hands together. Bob was sure something was wrong.

The coffee tasted good. As he sipped his joe, Brains thought of how he would explain what had happened. He needed his buddy's help desperately. Bob had proved to be a loyal friend in the past. For the past year while Brains was on *Bluefish*, Bob had been assigned to the tender. Boot camp at Great Lakes, Illinois, had first brought them together. One had chosen torpedoman "A" school in Orlando, Florida, and the other hull technician school in Philadelphia, Pennsylvania. Bob had gone on to diving school in Pearl Harbor, Hawaii. Eventually, they had both found a home in New London at the submarine school. Both were assigned to the operating squadron, one on subs and one on the tender, and they saw a lot of each other. The tender supervised the diving locker and the barge through the repair department. The R-6 division treated them as independent agents. As the two buddies talked, Brains softened the conversation by referring to home and school.

Finney talked about how he had come from New Mexico. It was unusual to find Navy men with roots in the Land of Enchantment. Finney's father, a retired naval officer, had told Bob to look at the sea service after high school. Finney didn't want to start in college right away. Mr. Clarence Finney had gone into land development and real estate after retiring from the Navy. He also had many avocations, including leather work, carpentry, and farming. He bought some prime land in the northeast corner of the state. Clarence and Gwendolyn, his wife of forty years, had developed a one thousand-acre ranch in a choice spot. The canyon around which they lived was beautiful. Aspens, firs, and many other varieties of flora abounded. Mountain lions, deer, coyotes, as well as birds of all description, were frequent visitors to their mountain retreat. Bob's mother and father had built a log cabin and added a shop and a barn. When he was last home, he discovered they had added a tennis court with a surface of sand and grass. It was easy on the knees. He had enjoyed fishing and swimming the man-made pond which his dad had built. Horses, burros, dogs, and ducks dotted the landscape and had to be fed routinely. Bob had told Brains how lucky his sister was to live in Albuquerque. She could remain at this paradise at seven thousand feet, which he was at sea level on the Long Island Sound. His sister, Janice, took her three girls to the country often. Bob and Brains laughed as they recalled the name of the burrito colt adopted from the US Government. Gwendolyn had named it "Taco Bell," because she said it made little burritos. With that, Brain took Bob into his confidence.

"Bob, I need your help." Bob listened and the more he heard, the wider open his mouth became. His face showed signs of utter disbelief to know Tom was dead. "You're my last resort, please...just tell me you'll help!" pleaded Brains.

"Tom...Tom Kozlowski, dead? When? Where? How? Tell me more about it! How can I help, except to hear you out?" was Bob's stunned reply.

"All I can say is we were together last night. He was using Stefan's car. Someone, I just got a quick glance at him in the dark...threw the keys of the car at me and told me not to look in the trunk until later. When I opened the trunk in the parking lot...there was Tom, blood all over, and his body was beginning to get stiff. Whoever killed him must have stuffed his body in the trunk while I was sleeping. When I left, without looking in the trunk, I parked the car near the rec center. Can you help me get rid of the body?"

Bob was beside himself. Astounded, to say the least. "Why didn't you just call the police and tell them what happened? You didn't kill Tom, did you?"

For whatever reason, Brains evaded an answer. Later, he was to discover why. He was describing the plans for hiding the body and didn't want to go on without getting a commitment from Bob,

Brains asked, "You'll have to tell me now, or I can't explain anymore. We don't have much time. Will you help me or not?"

Unwilling to take the final step in agreeing to assist him, Bob mumbled, "I probably will."

Brains continued. "I thought of all possible ways to make this the perfect crime. I think I've got it. The other day, Tom told me how much he hated sub duty. I'm sure CO or XO know about it. My guess is that when they discover him missing from muster, they'll assume he went UA. The fact that he had orders to another sub, when he wanted shore duty in the worst way, would make anyone go on unauthorized absence. His department head and division officer as well as compartment buddies knew he wanted to non-vol as a sub crewman. I was Tom's closest friend. He didn't like to get very close to anyone. He was sure acting funny and talking like I've never heard him before. Once he told me his folks died when he was just a little guy. He'd gone from one foster home to another, six in all before he was sixteen. Two of the families had abused him, beating him and locking him in the basement. All he did was talk back. I asked him if he knew who his real parents were. He told me his father had drowned when his lobster boat ran into some rocks in a storm on the rough Maine coastline. Tom told me he was born in Maine two years before his father died and that his mother had died during his birth. He had no brothers or sisters that he knew about."

Bob had heard enough. He interrupted and asked, "How do you think I can help?"

"Is that a promise to work with me? If it is, I'll go on to tell you what I have in mind. If not, forget it, nothing else will work and I might as well turn myself in. I'm in too deep, now."

Bob wanted to say he would, but again, he held back and simply said, "Just tell me what you've got up your sleeve, Brains."

Seemingly stuck with Bob's indecision, but still hopeful Bob would finally agree to help, Brains began to open up. Whether Bob would help or not didn't make much difference. Time was of the essence. Brains began to pour out his plan. "You'll have to take a big risk along with me. It might be difficult, but actually can work smoothly. You know, I'm qualified as a diver."

Bob tried to decipher the plan as he listened.

"It's 1700," Brains said. "We've got two and a half hours before I go back on watch. Duty chief gave me permission to go to the rec center. That's where they think I am now." Brains's mind was on fast track. "As I walked up to the car, I think I figured out a perfect way to get rid of the body. No one except you and me will ever know."

"Geez, Brains," said Finney, beginning to really back out. "What if I get a call from the tender? I'm here alone. I'm the duty driver. I'm on 'til 2000."

"Have you been called yet, today? Sunday's a slow day," prompted Brains.

"No...but anything could happen...that's what they tell us. What if there's another emergency?"

"Well," argued Brains, "first of all, we're the only sub in port. We're not going anywhere, 'cept in-activation. The tender certainly isn't going to call for a diver. I doubt they'll call you to shovel them out of the coffee grounds."

Bob was aware of the old joke that tenders are "an extension of the pier," "land-locked," or "never leave port because they're mired deep in the coffee grounds thrown over the side." But this was not a time for making jokes. "What are you driving at?" asked Finney, wishing he hadn't consented to help Brains this far. He looked at Brains's desperate face and Brains kept unfolding his unbelievable plan. Finney thought to himself, "Where is this easygoing, quiet, book-worm coming up with these wild ideas?" He knew of Brains's associates degree in criminology. His plans showed signs of genius, but Bob wasn't ready to fully commit himself…yet.

Brains got down to the meat of his plan. "Bob, all the diving gear we need is here. You taught me how to use all the stuff, right? Here's how we can get rid of Tom's body and commit the perfect crime."

Diver Finney's mouth dropped another inch as he heard the rest and, at that point, reluctantly agreed to help.

"We'll suit up, have everything on the repair raft, and ply our way around the tender," said Brains. "If anybody sees us, we're just doing a routine check. Nobody's going to recognize me in all that diver's get up. You know nobody ever checks these things out very carefully. They're supposed to, but, you know…"

"We don't need to dress up in diver's equipment just to throw the body in the Thames," thought Finney as he tried to read Brains's mind about his plan.

Brains had a different idea. He laid it all out. "Oh, the body will be covered by a canvas to look like part of the equipment. No one will see it in the dark, anyway. The weights will be around his ankles. See, Bob, *Bluefish* is leaving in ten days. No one is going under the boat between now and then. The last checks were made on Friday. As we go south through the Caribbean, sharks or other carnivorous fish will destroy the body. We have to sail through the Panama Canal, and from here to the Pacific will take two weeks."

Bob was beginning to see that Brains was ready to go through with his idea. "Have you figured some way to secure Tom's body to the boat? Sounds kinda' gross, Brains!"

Nothing was going to stop Brains now. "You've got plenty of line, I see. Tying the body will be a simple step. Once we have the body down, the lines we've tied to the hands and feet will be secured individually at two protrusions jetting out from the forward part of the ship."

"You mean the EM log sword and the sonar detection hydrophone?" Bob knew from working on putting in new speedometers that the EM log sword was one of the protrusions on the port side; the other, the SDH, was on the starboard side. "Are you sure the body could be tied there?" questioned Bob.

"Yeah, Tom's six feet tall. The distance between the two protrusions is more than that. The line will be around his wrists, which will give us the length we need."

"I can't believe it! Brains, you've thought of everything."

Brains took out a piece of paper from his heavy jacket. It was a diagram of the sub. It showed exactly where Tom would be tied. Bob stared at the paper. He looked at Brains quizzically but at that point gave his approval to help.

"Now what?" asked Bob.

"Let's get on with it. It's getting late."

CHAPTER SIXTEEN

IT TOOK EVERY OUNCE OF STRENGTH the two sailors could muster to move Tom's body down to the diving barge. Brains and Finney had taken along two one-by-six-inch planks, six feet long, to place under the stiffening body. A canvas covered it. Extra canvas was tucked at both ends to ensure no one could see what was inside. The boards would keep the limp body from sagging. As far as anyone knew, they were carrying supplies to the barge. The roving security patrol must have been elsewhere, as was the parking lot watch. As they lowered the body down the steps of the seawall to the barge, Finney tripped. His heart was pounding. If it hadn't been for the railing he would have fallen. They had carried the body face up, but now made sure it was face down inside the barge.

...

The phone rang. Brains held his breath as Bob answered. On the other end of the line was Bob's wife, Rachel.

"Where have you been? I've been trying to reach you for the last half hour," she remarked.

He was breathing heavily from the trip. As coolly as he could, he responded, "Honey, I've been picking up some gear for the crew tomorrow. Sure love you. Kind'a busy right now. I'll call back."

"Okay, sweets, just want you to know we love you. Baby just woke up for his feeding." Mikey was two months old, and Bob and Rachel's first child. "Wish you were home," added Rachel. "Guess you won't be back until Monday night, huh?"

"That's right, Babe. I'll see both of you, tomorrow. Give Mikey a big hug and kiss. Love you both. Bye!"

As they hung up, Bob breathed a sigh of relief, "Whew! That was close! Glad it was my wife and not the tender calling me out on a job.

That would have messed up what we're doing."

...

They began to put on their diving gear. That alone would have protected them against the chill and wind. Tom's body had begun to thaw. The water was warmer than the air. Together, those factors would make the job easier.

...

It was 1745. Brains didn't even stop to think that he was missing the evening meal. Finney mentioned it and they both knew they could get mid-rats, near 2000. The working barge was readied. They mentally checked off everything they needed. They were set to go.

The small 15 HP Mercury purred into action. They glided through the stillness of the dark night, illuminated by the light of the tender and the barge. Only the wind seemed to be against them. They avoided the tender's quarterdeck and watch because their location was starboard of the mother ship. No one else was out on the main deck in this weather. It was also chow time. Movies would be shown after chow, so they had luckily hit a good time. As they approached *Bluefish*, the top watch, Inter-Communication Technician Seaman Harold Buttrick, hearing the approach of the outboard, shined his flashlight in the direction of the sound.

"It's Guts," thought Brains. "I hope he's not on to anything, and doesn't ask any questions."

Guts hadn't received any instructions from the previous watch regarding work to be done. He recognized the Diving Repair Barge. He shrugged his shoulders. Inexperience, perhaps, kept him from questioning the event. It was 1755. He knew he had to write every occurrence in the log. He wrote, "1755—diving repair barge with two divers aboard. Permission requested and granted to work under *Bluefish*'s bow and EM log sword." At 1800, he wrote the routine entry, "Secure." He went back to thinking about the magazine that was still under his pillow.

Finney and Brains, working feverishly, tied the barge to the pier on the sub's port side, then dove in with Tom's body between them. They moved clumsily. The water seemed warmer than they first thought. The weights pulled Tom away, but miraculously they managed to hold the body in position. No one had suspected anything. The salt water made tying the heavy load easier. They had tied Tom's body to the underside of the sub in record time.

As they emerged from the ocean again, Guts flashed his light in their direction.

Diver Finney called out, "Repair accomplished!"

Guts logged the comment down at 1834. It had taken them only thirty-four minutes to take care of their unbelievable effort. The top watch kept his eye on the barge 'til it went around the tender. Brains did not speak or let his face be seen. Guts would surely have recognized him. But Guts, on the deck of *Bluefish*, simply went back to fantasizing about his next adventure. He couldn't wait for his next liberty.

Brains and Bob pulled in to the diving barge's mooring and tied up. Once in the shack, they changed out of their wet suits and made sure everything was back in place. The coffee tasted good. They both warmed themselves up. The outside temperature was twenty-three degrees.

"That was easier than I thought!" said Brains, a ton of worry off his mind. "Bob, you've been a real friend. I'll do anything for you...anytime."

Finney was just glad it was all over. He was glad to see Brains off to the *Bluefish*. In a way, he hoped he'd never see him again.

He called his wife. "Rachel, darlin', just wanted to tell you and Mikey I love you. I sure miss you!"

As they hung up, Rachel detected a note of nervousness in his voice. He didn't seem himself.

It was 2005 and Finney had been relieved by the oncoming watch. He went to the tender's berthing compartment to lay on his rack. All he wanted to do was sleep and forget what he had just done.

CHAPTER SEVENTEEN

IT WAS EARLY MONDAY MORNING. Ensign Palmer had a room at the bachelor officers' quarters when he didn't stay aboard. He drove to his sub and greeted the 2400-0800 top watch in his usual friendly manner and by first name. "How are things, Jud?"

Engineman seaman Judson Perry returned the greeting with the double salute to reply to the ensign.

"Morning, Mr. Palmer, sir. All A.O.K., sir!" It was 0630. "Lots of work today, sir?"

"Always. Got to keep on top of things!"

Daylight saving time made dawn come early but it was still hard to see without lights. Palmer disappeared down the lit mid-hatch into the sub. His body was still sore from the lessons he had been talked into by his BOQ-mate, Ensign Clark "Smilin" Jack Orr. Palmer had wanted to play racquet ball but Clark had talked him into tennis. The tennis pro had charged them forty-five dollars for two lessons. He wondered whether sore arms, tired legs, and a blister on his right hand after using a borrowed racquet was worth it.

Ensign Palmer was a sportsman. Sailing was his number one sport. He used the facilities at the submarine base marina. It had all the equipment he needed. He couldn't wait for the weather to break and the water sports season to open in April. He was almost sure he'd be assigned to another sub out of New London. He didn't get much time to work on his 240Z Datsun, which he liked to keep in pristine condition. He made sure he kept a tarp over it when it was not in use. The hobby shop automotive garage was a favorite place for him to spend off hours. His car was admired by all. There was never a speck of oil or tar on it. Polishing was a must. Palmer was an extremely responsible officer.

Studying the systems on a submarine was foremost among his priorities, now. He was anxious for those gold dolphins.

Both his mother and father back in St. Louis shared in his accomplishments. They had come to Newport to the graduation at the Officers Candidate School. His time at OCS with Smiling Jack had opened up new friendships and fun activities, like sailing, for them. The Black Pearl restaurant in Newport's famous shopping area and the almost full meal clam chowder drew them there. The first time he'd been there was to jointly celebrate with both sets of parents at graduation. When Jonathan's dad made one of his business trips for American Can to New York and stopped over for a few days, that had been a special time. Palmer's mother, independent from the word go, was a criminal lawyer. She went by her maiden name, Claire Cummings, and had aspired to become the next representative to the US Congress from her district. She was sure to win. Letters from her came to Jonathan on a weekly basis and were usually typewritten, a sign of her personality, always neat and proper. The last one he read indicated that her legal practice was growing and that she was doing rather well in her campaign for the House.

Palmer made his way into the wardroom. He was alone at this early hour. The wardroom mess specialist took his order. Jonathan filled his cup of coffee. Soon, Custer, or "Fred," as Palmer knew him when the other officers were not around, brought his breakfast. Sugar and cream were placed beside him. "Last Stand," as Custer was known, also knew that Palmer couldn't stand Navy coffee when it was black. Most sailors liked it strong. The standing joke was that coffee was made from dirty socks that had been worn for a week at a time. Palmer liked his coffee, as hardened sailors would say, "sissy style" with cream and sugar. But Custer was well-liked by the officers because he knew each of their preferences. He made sure they were well fed. If he could persuade the chief cook to prepare surf and turf twice a week, he would do it. Officers preferred to eat aboard on those nights. Food on submarines was definitely the best in all the Services. The Navy, and certainly *Bluefish*'s cooks, did not scrimp on anything.

More officers appeared as Palmer dug into his French toast, orange juice, and coffee. In a few minutes, their freedom would be directed at being officers of *Bluefish*. They would have to put everything else out of their minds. One of them grumbled about his unlucky plight over the weekend.

"Damn car broke down right on the main drag on Route 12. Cost me $400 and messed up the whole weekend."

"Humph," chimed in another. "You had it easy. Better stay single! When I got home Friday, I found a note inside the front door. The wife had left with our two kids. The call to her Friday morning, to inform her of my order to stay on *Bluefish* 'til its inactivation and go with the sub to Washington State, didn't set well with her. She packed a few things and went back to Georgia. She said she couldn't take another separation. 'It's the Navy or me,' she said. She called last night from Atlanta. Either I go there or else she's suing for divorce."

Everyone shook their heads in disbelief. This was not the usual slow Monday. Everything had to be checked. There were only eight days left before the sail to Bremerton. The call to quarters sounded.

It was too cold to muster top side. Each division mustered with its leading petty officer at 0720. Several chiefs were division officers, as was Ensign Palmer, and Steve Champion from Princeton, New Jersey. He met with his division, made up of torpedomen, amongst the ship's weapons. Everyone was accounted for except Kozlowski. No one was surprised.

...

Torpedoman First Class Thomas G. Kozlowski had openly talked with several in his division and other crewmembers of jumping ship. He really disliked the Navy. Every time his department head, Lieutenant Clifford Brandish, a Southerner from South Carolina, talked to him about being late, he swore he would not come back that very night. He had never made good his threat. The last time he was late, Brandish warned him that he would go on report, which meant having to appear at captain's mast, the Navy's non-judicial punishment action. Instead, Lieutenant Brandish had given him extra duty. He could apply this punishment as a department head. That kept Tom from having an official record of misbehavior. It was not much more than a slap on the wrist and it would keep Kozlowski from going off the ship on liberty on a non-duty night. Most of the torpedomen expected him to come in late, dragging his feet from heavy drinking and a heavy date.

...

The men huddled among the Mark 4 torpedoes, which were all secure. The torpedoes looked ominous though unarmed. They could carry nuclear warheads. If so, one of these "fish" could easily obliterate the largest enemy vessel or, aimed properly, could wipe out an entire seacoast for miles.

Moving the torpedoes around for storing and firing was only a problem of correct identification. Everything was computerized, unlike the back-breaking work it had taken to store and prepare torpedoes for firing on World War II diesel subs like *Halibut* or *Finnback*, or other subs of naval history. They had required the strength of seven men working seventeen hours a day to prepare them. There would be no electrically powered hoists.

Now, they easily moved these sophisticated weapons on well-lubricated metal rollers. The operators were all especially trained for many weeks to respond to any emergency that might require their use. The torpedo was the main weapon system of the Sturgeon class submarine. They had to be inspected regularly by well-trained men in the weapons department aboard the tender. It was obvious how careful they had to be as you entered the compartment. The cleanliness of their spaces and their impeccable uniforms were marks of the torpedoman. No lint or dust in the mechanism could ever be tolerated. They were taught from the start that no mistake was permissible in a possible engagement with any adversary.

Following the division muster, a muster took place in front of the executive officer. As the division officers headed up, Brains said loud enough for him to hear, "Guess, Tom's alarm didn't go off."

...

"Tom's a snake-ranch artist!" called out a senior chief. He knew what that was all about.

Senior Chief Torpedoman Harte lowered his head. He had been caught in the trap of having a "snake ranch." As a result, his family had gone through a break-up since his last Far East tour out of Hawaii. He'd been able to spend four months in Yokohama, most of which was spent in the company of a Japanese mistress. He hadn't given much thought to his snake-ranch episode until his transfer to *Bluefish* months later. He had left his wife back home in Cheyenne with his teenage children. The purpose of the visit to Wyoming was for his wife, Sarah, to visit her aging and ill mother while he was on an unaccompanied duty overseas. He had called her regularly. Two years ago, after his Japanese tour, he and his family had moved to Groton. During a patrol on *Bluefish*, Senior Torpedoman Chief Harte's wife became curious about a letter from someone named Michiko Maruoka. It was obviously from the "Land of the Rising Sun." She opened it. It contained a picture of Michiko dressed in a beautiful Japanese formal costume. A second picture showed a little boy, not more than a year-and-a-half old. The letter, in broken English, said, "Emile, my heart, little Glenn-san and I anxious you send for us. Please write me." Sarah had glued the envelope back together with the letter inside. The steaming which she had used to open it had not torn the flap. When Emile came back from patrol he opened the letter, but said nothing. On the next telephone bill there was a call to Yokohama. She asked him about it. They had a fight. He insisted it had been made to a buddy. She knew then that he wasn't to be trusted. Several weeks later, Sarah and the two children moved to Cheyenne.

As Senior Chief Torpedoman Harte thought of his own life, he felt sorry for Tom, who was perhaps caught up in this same web. "I hope things turn out better for him," Harte mused.

CHAPTER EIGHTEEN

ENSIGN PALMER BUMPED into one of his men as he was returning from the XO's stateroom. Third Class Randy K. Thomas seemed to be emotionally distraught. To show emotion was not common among submariners, especially aboard the boat. Randy was a seasoned sailor. Palmer pulled him aside in the narrow passageway. "Hey, man, what's the long face for? Cheer up, it couldn't be all that bad."

"But it is," responded Randy. "Sorry, sir!" he said almost at once. "I guess I just don't know what to do anymore. I've been working on this application for discharge for reason of conscientious objection for so long, I'm about to give up. I've followed all the procedures to the letter. He just refuses to see me," uttered Randy, tearfully. He tried to regain his composure before the ensign.

Palmer had seen a physical change come over Thomas in the last six months. His mental attitude, in particular, was disturbing to the executive officer. He was not only hurting the morale of those on *Bluefish*, but Thomas's open disdain for the Naval Establishment had become totally negative. The ensign knew that one of these days the XO would make good his threat to court-martial Thomas. Thomas had refused to do his work as a quartermaster on several occasions. When it came close to being put on report, he did just enough work to prevent that. Another minute on each occasion of not doing what he was ordered would have constituted "dereliction of duty."

Another obvious and glaring reality was Thomas's appearance. He was letting his hair grow longer than regulations allowed. In addition, he now wore wire-framed glasses with small lenses. His regulation, "squared away" shipmates called him a peacenik, a rebel. He began to be assigned jobs like cleaning the heads or being a gopher. In derision, they called him "Colonel of the Urinal" or "Captain of the Head." He was no longer using his quartermaster skills, working with the electronic technicians on SINS and plotting and charting.

The executive officer, LCDR Ivan Scott, who had relieved Pappy had no room for Thomas's kind. He felt he had to get a job done and was frustrated by having to spend his time on malcontents. He was initially angered by the insinuations in Thomas's application that the *Bluefish* was a "war machine." XO was convinced, as were most submariners, that the Sub Force was a "deterrent force for peace." The Department of Defense would not disagree. Thomas had felt that way at one time. XO's point was that Thomas had received the government's money for three years, taxpayers' money, to be trained, and for all the benefits he had received, now had the gall to back out on his commitment. He had let Thomas speak briefly during their first encounter about his application.

Their conversation started out when Thomas said, "XO, sir, I've served three years of a six-year term, honorably. I've done what I was told and I believe I've earned my pay. But my religious beliefs have undergone a change in the last few months. I don't honestly believe there is room for war of any kind. This submarine is a weapon. I'm riding a weapon. We carry nuclear warheads on our torpedoes. I don't want to ride on an undersea time bomb anymore. I don't want to be an accomplice for killing millions of people, not to speak of the devastation to the rest of God's creation."

The executive officer had politely, but you could tell on his reddening face that he was furious, asked him to leave his stateroom. "Go talk to the chaplain, again. Maybe he can set you straight," he remarked to the confused sailor.

Randy was now in his fourth try at getting his application to pass the XO's screening, and confided in Palmer, fighting back the tears.

"XO said I was a yellow-bellied, gutless, stupid excuse for a man," Thomas told Palmer. "He said I was letting my countrymen down. And then he brought up my folks in West Virginia. He said I should have stayed back there and mined coal with the rest of my kind. Said they cower back there in those hills and that I'll see that things aren't like I say they are. He said I've wasted people's time. He promised to burn me, Palmer. He meant it! I could tell by the fury in his voice."

Palmer understood what Thomas was saying. He had heard the XO make this kind of threat to others. It worked in some cases. Palmer seriously felt this approach was uncalled for in this instance. He thought, "Sure the submarine force needs men, but why make them go through hell if it's a volunteer outfit?" All the officers knew how difficult it was for enlisted men to non-volunteer.

Randy was hurt by the fact that the XO had brought his family and West Virginia folks into the discussion He knew them only as the best of American citizens. Hard work was a part of their daily life. In his family, he was the middle son of six children. His mother, whom he called "Ma," was in a hospital. She'd been diagnosed with tuberculosis, rare now, but still occurring where difficult living conditions existed. Ma had sacrificed her food for her children and worked hard to give them what they had. The poverty that ran rampant in the hills did not permit his mother to have the household appliances that would have made her chores easier. Randy's father couldn't hold a job, or was laid off, often. Yet the Thomas family maintained a strong religious faith. Ma had insisted that all the brood attend church. He had gone on Sunday morning and evening and on Wednesdays until he was thirteen. Then, to help feed those still at home, he started working full-time after school and on weekends at a restaurant off the expressway. He walked three miles there and three miles back home.

When he was a junior in the regional high school, some Navy recruiters had stopped for breakfast one weekend. They were good at what they did. Their sales pitch sounded attractive. Randy was tired of scrimping, and when the recruiters told him the Navy would treat him very well, he was impressed.

"I'm having to support my family," he had interjected into their pitch. "My older brothers and sisters are married."

They persuaded him by saying that he would make more money in the Navy and could still support his family by sending money home regularly. "An allotment from your paycheck would go home every month, Randy," they clarified.

When he told his folks about it, his father objected. His mother put her hand on his head, in the form of a blessing, and quietly said, "Do what you have to do, son."

Thomas had gone down to the Charleston Navy Recruiting Station and was greeted by the two recruiters who had talked him into joining. The next day he was on the way to the Orlando Naval Training Center. Boot camp was not like working in a restaurant off Interstate 64 near his home in Thurmond.

At boot camp, he remembered attending chapel on Sundays. It was a good way to escape from the incessant yelling and screaming by the petty officers in charge in the squad bays. The chapel gave him time to think. One day, the chaplain's sermon was about perseverance. It helped him get through the next phase and eventually through boot camp. He had wanted to run away several times. He said to himself that if others had been able to survive through tough times, he could, too. He bit his lower lip and kept going.

Graduation was a final relief. He was given orders to Quartermaster "A" School at the Schools Command at Orlando; he did well, especially in mathematics, which was his strength, and finished first in his class. As a result he was promoted to third class. While at "A" school, he took the General Education Development Test, passed it and was promised a high school diploma. All the success had made his stay in the Navy, at that point, worthwhile. He felt the Navy was good for him and was glad he'd overcome the desire to go UA.

While on leave after "A" school, he went to church with his father and younger brother. The Pentecostal minister whom he had known for many years greeted him warmly. The town of Thurmond was small and everyone came from all nooks and crannies of the hills to attend the sermons. Church was one of the big social events of the week. People filled up the small wooden sanctuary. During his pastoral prayer, Pastor Flemington mentioned Randy's name. A phrase he used stuck in Thomas's mind and wouldn't leave him. He had said, "Oh, God, make Randy a peacemaker as well as a peacekeeper." Thomas appreciated that acceptance of his role, but it bothered him. He wished he knew why.

...

Shortly after reporting to *Bluefish*, Randy had talked with several people. Ensign Jonathan Palmer had been one of them. He remembered that Palmer had said he should see others who had a variety of opinions. Following that advice, he accepted the fact that everyone he saw emphasized their point of view strongly, some in favor of his becoming a conscientious objector, while others thought he was ill-informed. The greatest majority were non-committal and seemed to favor the idea of letting Randy make up his own mind. Those at the counseling center that helped CO cases in Stonington were convinced that "Nukes" were an invention of the devil. Randy disliked radical approaches and looked for a sane approach. Palmer had led him to understand this was the best approach—and he sought an objective point of view.

He'd heard and knew that if you had a problem, the chaplain is a good one to share that frustration with. He had dropped in unexpectedly on the tender chaplain one afternoon. It turned out to be a good move, as he later thought of it. He hadn't made up his mind to apply for discharge as a "conscientious objector."

"Chaplain, I'm bothered by my role as a crewmember aboard a submarine," Thomas began.

The chaplain sensed this might be a long conversation. He made sure

Randy was comfortable and, after hearing him out, responded.

"Randy," he said (the young sailor liked his personal approach), "did you know there is an official route to being classified as a conscientious objector?"

"No, sir."

The chaplain took out a copy of the Bureau of Naval Personnel Manual article on the subject. "I'll make a copy of this for you. Come by tomorrow and my religious program specialist will have it for you in the ship's library. As you know, it's across the passageway."

Being inside the chaplain's office, and also his stateroom, was comforting. It was definitely a private situation. The fact that the chaplain was given the right not to reveal anything inside of those four walls, called "privileged communication," was helpful for Randy to know. The chaplain had advised him of that.

"Randy, once you start this process, however, it's like being branded. There's no removing the scar, no turning back. That's for your sake as well as the Navy's." Using a hackneyed expression, the chaplain went on, "It's like being pregnant, either you are or you're not. Can't be a little bit that way, you know! You have a tough subject to deal with. History is replete with examples of persons who have gone either the way of fighting back for what they believe, or practicing non-violence. When you're already wearing the uniform of your country, it isn't easy to go the non-violent route. When you raised your hand to enlist, you agreed to defend your country. I have yet to find someone who is absolutely interested in making war, or out to kill someone for the sake of destroying life. I have no doubt that there are some in this world who are bent on destroying everything in their sight. Dysfunctional people, right from the start." Looking straight at Randy, the chaplain said, "You must remember that you can't use God or the Bible to get you out of tight places. This real world just isn't that way. You can get out of a tight places by letting God lead you, but you have to make certain it is a higher power than your own pushing you in that direction. To put it bluntly, hard work and a lot of perspiration will have to come from you. You might want to finish out your commitment. How many years have you got left on this hitch?"

"A little over three, sir," said Randy, blinking. Randy was entranced by the chaplain's understanding when he listened, and in his confidence when he spoke.

The chaplain continued, "If whenever you decide you want to go the conscientious objector direction, know that, though it may appear that many are in your way, you'll have to keep moving ahead. It'll take every ounce of perseverance and patience you can muster. It may cost you greatly."

The advice sounded very much like what the chaplain at Orlando had said, when he had helped Thomas persevere through boot camp.

"I might add," the padre began to conclude, "that you had better start developing a mighty tough outer crust as well as a tolerant spirit. Being the laughing stock among your peers isn't easy. I just want you to know, now, that whatever your decision is, I'll stand by you. I have learned not to judge. You can rest assured everything we have talked about is kept between us. But remember, the same God that has stuck by your ma through her illness is at your side, and by the side of all creation. Truth can be seen from many perspectives."

Randy remembered that the chaplain asked him to spend some moments in prayer. He felt a sense of peace. Here, aboard a warship, though mostly a mother ship which was a "repair and supply base" for submarines, he was comforted. He knew that his submarine, one of eight in the operating squadron, had just come back from patrolling the lanes of the sea, carrying weapons that could mean the end of millions of lives if their action started a nuclear war. Yet, here he was feeling as though the Creator of the Universe had a say in all of this. For a slight second, he was warmed by the thought that the controlling force behind all the planets and stars and galaxies in the macro-cosmos was in fact more powerful than all the nuclear warheads amassed in all the stockpiles of all the nations of the world. He left the tender with new resolve to make a definite decision to finish his enlistment, or try for a discharge.

...

"Thanks for sharing with me your experience with the chaplain," Palmer told Randy. "Keep that to yourself, for now. In fact, through this next patrol, don't breathe any word of this to anyone. If you do, it'll get out and you'll be branded as a sea lawyer, or just be blamed for wanting to get out of going on another patrol."

Randy had agreed. He was not about to make waves, now.

...

Eight months later, Thomas applied for a discharge By Reason of Conscientious Objection. That was the time XO had all but thrown Thomas out bodily from his stateroom and had belittled him. Randy had applied after his talks with Palmer and the chaplain and spent the last patrol doing his job.

...

The discussion with Palmer had included the merits of a non-violent approach to living.

Randy remembered what he had told Palmer. "I know how complex our world is. Well, I'm beginning to know. Back in West Virginia, it seemed easier to see and feel close to God. Mountains and hills were all around me. I remember going to the lake at Babcock State Park and feeling a kinship with all the animals, birds, and fish. I'd get a thrill each morning, just waking up, even though I knew Ma was sick and Dad was without work. Whether the sun came up over the hill or the day was cloudy, rainy, or miserably cold from snow or sleet, I'd feel good. Whenever people would bad-mouth God, even as a kid, it made me wonder how people could do that. Since coming into the Navy, Mr. Palmer, everything has been so different. Why, I ask myself, are people mad at the very power that gives them breath?"

Palmer had listened attentively and gave an acknowledging nod.

Thomas continued, "Is there a reason for me to question the type of leadership that moves toward violence? How are we helping the world find peace by providing weapons for small nations to destroy themselves? Is it right to have people living in luxury while others starve? What keeps a nation, wealthy by comparison to all others, from ensuring the welfare of all? What makes it so hard for our own citizens to help each other?"

Palmer knew that Randy was struggling.

"I see children on TV, stomachs bloated. No one should be dying for lack of food. The homeless, the illiterate, the poor in general—seeing and knowing all of that really gets to me. Mr. Palmer, I want to wear this uniform proudly, but I've also got to care for those I say I defend. I find I'm just doing the opposite. I feel like a hypocrite. I can't keep being false to myself."

Palmer thought of his college course on Shakespeare when he heard Randy. He recalled the passage from *Hamlet* in which Polonius says to his son Laertes, "This above all: to thine own self be true, And it must follow, as the night the day, Thou canst then not be false to any man..."

"You've asked a lot of deep questions," he said to Thomas. "Humanity has been asking themselves these same questions for a long time. Don't expect any special treatment from your shipmates if you decide on a discharge application." Moving on, he asked, "Randy, what would you do with your life, if you got out?"

"Now you've got me, Mr. Palmer. I'd finish college, for one thing. I've been paying into the G.I. Bill. Maybe I could be an advocate for those in need. Maybe I could become a lawyer and try to influence legislation as a political figure that would move our country into a better relationship with the rest of the world." That answer seemed to win Palmer's approval.

...

The patrol had gone well, and now after several attempts made by

Thomas at submitting his application only to have it be rejected by the XO, Palmer agreed to go back to the executive officer. He wasn't going to let a good man down. As Palmer approached the XO's stateroom, he heard a commotion.

CHAPTER NINETEEN

THE PASSAGEWAY IN OFFICERS' COUNTRY was crowded. Ensign Palmer, who was on his way to see the XO about Thomas's Conscientious Objector application, was surprised to hear Thomas called over the boat's inter-communication system (1MC). Among the enlisted crewmen nervously standing "at ease" with their hands clasped behind their backs and their feet a foot apart were ETSN Buttrick, TM2 D'Cenzo and one man Palmer didn't recognize. He later discovered it was a diver, off the tender, HT2 Robert W. Finney. Guts seemed to be the only one really at ease. Thomas came running after he heard his name, saw the ensign there, and smiled broadly. He would be in for a surprise.

In a matter of minutes, each of the men had been seen briefly by Naval Investigative Services Officers. The NIS agents, dressed in civilian clothes, were actually active duty types, undercover cops for the Navy. They read each sailor their rights: "You're reminded that anything you say can be used against you in a court of law." The first part of the Fifth Amendment sank in: "You may choose to remain silent."

As Guts was being escorted into the wardroom for the longer interview, Palmer had slipped Thomas's Conscientious Objector application, almost book-length, into the XO's incoming basket. XO had left his stateroom door open after talking with the NIS. He turned toward Palmer and seemed to explode. Thomas, D'Cenzo, and Finney couldn't quite make sense of his venom toward Ensign Palmer.

"You just don't have any more damn gray matter than this excuse for a man!" he yelled at Palmer, and as he looked at Thomas, who was reporting in after being called on the 1MC. "Look at him," the XO went on, pointing at Thomas and directing his remarks at Palmer. "He may be a murderer."

Palmer and Thomas exchanged quizzical glances.

"God damn it, Palmer. You make me as sick, as does this jerk!" shouted the XO. "Why don't you just go back to your division and run it like you're supposed to? Stay out of my sight! Our first priority is to get this boat ready for in-activation. Now this mess...!" He was referring to the sudden involvement with the investigation which brought the NIS on the scene. "This damn investigation, plus some other stupid, over the weekend unauthorized activity, and you have the gall to bring this crap in to me? Wake up, lame brain!"

The rage in the young ensign's face at being called on the carpet, especially before the enlisted crewmen, was too much. It was followed by Jonathan's move into the XO's stateroom. He closed the door behind him. He'd had enough from this "book" man. "You need to run a tight ship," he thought, "but not at my expense. Whatever the problems are, this guy's got them."

"Don't close the door unless I order you to!" shouted the XO, startled at the ensign's bravado. His surprise was increased as Ensign Palmer continued to stand against the closed door, his hand on the knob. Jonathan started to speak in quiet tones, his lips stretching, his words deliberate.

"I'm through taking it, XO. A man can only take so much. Request permission to see the commanding officer. But before I see him, I have something to say to you. I don't know what your problem is. Everyone on this boat hates your guts."

The XO, a man of considerable size, interrupted, "Shut up! I'm not here to win a popularity contest with you or anyone else. Might be best if you keep your thoughts to yourself."

Jonathan went on, "I'm not finished. I hope you awaken to the fact that the only things that make a sub operate are people. No matter how young or inexperienced, everyone has to be treated with respect and dignity. You haven't done that, unless you've wanted to win points with someone more senior to you. What makes you so sour and foul-mouthed all the time? In spite of the great accomplishment of this sub, brought about by people, there's enough anger on this boat toward you to cause an explosion. I haven't been aboard very long, but long enough to be brought to a boil. Only one example of your callousness has been your unwillingness to give Thomas a proper hearing. You keep sending him back with his application for more review without even looking at it. This is the fourth time that I've brought it to your attention. It should be sent up the chain of command. I venture to say that the captain hasn't even heard of his request. I'm fed up! My conversation with the CO will be to present my observations of your conduct and to tender my resignation. I've had it!"

With eyebrows raised, Lieutenant Commander Ivan Scott rolled his chair back. He had decided to sit down during Palmer's onslaught. His hands, clasped together behind his neck, tightened. He felt his whole body perspiring. It wasn't often that a junior officer talked this way to a senior. He tried to be calm though his face showed redness.

"Very well, Ensign Palmer, I'll inform you when you can see the captain. Just want you to know that your man is one of the prime suspects in a murder of one of our crew. His paperwork as a Conscientious Objector will have to wait until after the investigation."

Palmer, in his anger, had momentarily forgotten that Thomas was referred to as a possible murderer. Palmer suddenly turned pale.

...

The facts had spread like wildfire that a body had been discovered strapped to *Bluefish*'s underside. Soon after muster, XO had checked the log of the weekend's activities. LCDR Scott, a perfectionist and a "by the book" officer, was commendable in some regards, but it grated on some of his juniors.

Ivan Scott had been this way most of his life. His father, a physician, and his mother, a career librarian, had instilled their values in him early. He had been a precocious child, excelling in academics at every level in school. He was a one-woman man, and he and Julie had three lovely children, all top students in East Lyme schools. Ivan preferred reading to watching television. The *New York Times* Sunday edition, with its Magazine and Book Review sections, was his favorite weekly item when he was in port. His wife made sure they were mailed or kept on hand, especially the *Times* crossword puzzle. Scott had graduated from the University of Illinois. His father had insisted he take NROTC. That had gotten him started in thinking about marine engineering, and when he graduated he received his commission as an ensign and a well-deserved bachelor of science. His choice of the submarine service was a coincidence. The Navy's need for officers in this community was well advertised. After a short orientation course at Newport Naval Base in Rhode Island, he had gone to Officer's Basic Submarine School in Groton. He wasn't sure that they listed the Sub Base in New London, but found out that before Groton had a post office, there was no other way to get mail except through New London, and the address still included the name, New London. Scott received an MBA, which was followed by his attending Naval postgraduate school in Monterrey, California. He had come to *Bluefish* as a department head and had assumed the role as executive officer a year ago. The former XO had received message orders to Washington's 0-2 office at the Pentagon.

...

Earlier, in his usual fashion, Scott had scoured the entries in the top watch log for the weekend. He had become aware of the problems of Commander Blair's son and his friends on Sunday afternoon, so the entry concerning that interruption of the routine was noted and understood. CO had with some embarrassment shared the results with him at 0700. As his eyes assiduously looked down the log, he had seen what he thought were questionable entries. The person on watch had been ETSN Buttrick. His initials were by each entry. At 1745 there had been an "All Secure" entry. The next was to have been at 1800.

In between was one that caught his eye. It read: "1755—Diving Repair Barge with two divers aboard. Permission requested and granted to work under *Bluefish*'s bow and EM Log Sword." The 1800 entry was "All Secure." As he read further, 1815 and 1830 entries were similar. At 1834 ETSN Buttrick had logged, "Repair by divers completed and acknowledged."

In a flash, XO had called the commanding officer, the OOD who'd been on duty Sunday and the navigation department head. They had discussed the entries, all agreeing that no work on *Bluefish*'s bow had been authorized. The phone rang off the hook in both Repair and diving barge only to confirm that no repairs on *Bluefish* were logged in their records. Commander Blair was on the horn to the repair officer, Commander Salisbury, as ETSN Buttrick appeared at the request of XO. He was immediately questioned about the entries, barely having time to go in among the four officers who crowded the small room.

Buttrick began to try to explain, "Two divers on the repair barge approached and told me they were checking the EM sword log for problems, and assuming all was in order I let them go on."

The officers couldn't believe what they were hearing from Buttrick.

"Are you saying that you didn't check their story with anyone? Not even the OOD or the chief of the watch?" asked the captain incredulously.

"No, sir, I assumed the squadron had ordered the check. I just figured they knew," said, Buttrick nervously. "Why are you asking? Did I do something wrong?"

"First of all, don't use the word 'assume.' Assuming in this business is putting an ass between you and me. That doesn't fly! You may be in for a lot of trouble. Security is top priority. You don't do anything without checking it out with higher authority."

...

Only a few knew of the captain's own predicament regarding his son's incident aboard *Bluefish*. The squadron commander had not responded favorably to that, and now this incident was happening. The heat of the squadron commander's ire would surely increase. ETSN Buttrick was turned over to the investigators.

...

After the log entries were read, an all-hands evolution took place. The diving barge was soon in place, made its look-see beneath the boat and, discovering a body, brought it to the surface. Reality had replaced the rumor that had gone throughout the boat. Shock and disbelief were visible on every sailor's face. No incident like this had ever happened in the submarine force. Every sailor was later to find out the details of the bizarre scheme. And ambulance from the sub base was waiting to take the now-identified body of TM1 Thomas G. Kozlowski's corpse. The ambulance rushed away. The entire crew was petrified by what had been found, especially the weapon's department personnel, and they moved slowly to their assigned spaces, disturbed by this unheard-of act.

By 0900, NIS agents were on board. The prime suspects had been lined up outside the wardroom. They had been read their rights and the interviewing had begun with Buttrick, who had been put on report for false log entries and not reporting the diving barge request to higher authority. His questioning over, Thomas had been called in. Finney and D'Cenzo exchanged knowing glances as they saw Thomas go into the wardroom.

"Why did you kill Kozlowski?" the investigators asked Thomas. They were anxious for a confession. "You sure had this all planned out, didn't you? We got you all figured out. The XO put us wise to you. You wanted to be transferred to the tender! UA was also part of your plan, wasn't it? Well, don't plan on it. Now spill it!"

Before QM3 Thomas could answer there was a knock on the wardroom door. *Bluefish*'s skipper pushed MM1 Charles L. Connolly, in handcuffs, toward them. An armed sentry accompanied him.

Commander Blair informed the investigators, "I think this is your man. Sorry for interrupting. Just got a report from the hospital that they're performing an autopsy. We just caught this man trying to deep six this piece of evidence, a .38 Special."

The gun, wrapped in a plastic bag, was laid on the conference table. Cowboy was ordered to take a seat. He looked confused. His comment reflected his fear, as well. "I didn't do anything." He didn't want to reveal his original intentions to shoot a former instructor from submarine school. He hadn't bargained that his actions with the .38 would get him into this mess, regarding Tom's death. "I'll be more than glad to answer your questions," he told the NIS investigators.

While looking over the record of QM3 Thomas's activities over the weekend, the investigators discovered that he had not been off *Bluefish* in the last seventy-two hours. He could not have been involved in the murder. He had spent the time preparing the final draft of his essay to be included in his application as a Conscientious Objector. NIS let him go with the admonition, "Don't go too far, and stay aboard. We may need you later."

Thomas left, feeling as though a weight had been lifted.

CHAPTER TWENTY

AS HT1 FINNEY WALKED NERVOUSLY into the wardroom, Cowboy, who had just undergone the investigators' grilling, brushed past him. He heard the investigators say to the guard, "Keep him under strict surveillance."

No matter where Cowboy tried to make himself scarce inside the sub, he felt his shipmates' eyes watching him. Word spreads fast in a submarine. They all knew that Cowboy had tried to ditch a .38 overboard. No further investigation was needed as far as they were concerned to tie him to TM1 Kozlowzki's murder. They had all liked Tom's jovial spirit. Now he lay at the Submarine Base Hospital's Medical Center, forever silenced. Cowboy would pay for his crime.

The senior investigator, Parham, and his assistant, Duvalle, both active members of the Armed Forces and submariners, spoke quietly to each other as HT1 Finney sat down. With a hand covering his mouth, Parham said, referring to Cowboy, "We've got the murderer—just give these next two a going over they'll never forget!" Duvalle smiled, knowingly.

Finney recounted the procedure involved in strapping Tom's body to the underside of the sub's bow. The investigators' faces revealed their amazement. The whole scheme had almost worked, except for an alert XO who had read the log. Parham and Duvalle marveled at how anyone could have thought of using the EM log sword containing the speedometer and the active sonar detection hydrophone extension. It was an ingenious plan, to use the only two possible protrusions at a distance enough between them to tie the body.

"I was only doing my buddy, Brains, TM2 Julian D'Cenzo, a favor, honestly," was Finney's frightened statement, as he concluded his story. Brains had told Finney to tell it all just as it happened. It didn't sound made up to the investigators. He was definitely an accomplice.

"Stay at the divers' barge. No, on second thought, belay that."

They called the repair officer, Commander Salisbury. He agreed to supply a guard and take Finney to the crew's lounge next to the chaplain's office and the ship's library on the sub tender. They made sure the repair officer understood that Finney was to be guarded carefully.

The NIS men consulted with one another before Brains was called in. HT1 Finney's story was changing the picture. They agreed to be very careful in questioning the next suspect.

As they heard D'Cenzo, he corroborated Finney's story. Finney had told how he and Brains hauled the body from the IROC-Z to the Barge. He even revealed the false job order for repairs beneath *Bluefish* in case they were confronted. He explained how they had tied weights to the body in case it was dislodged. The body would surely sink if it hadn't been devoured by sharks or other fish. D'Cenzo did not change any of the story. The two, Finney and D'Cenzo, had not had enough time, since they were called up, to concoct a similar story; this was the thought going through the minds of both NIS investigators. Their dilemma now was how to connect MM1 Charles L. Connolly, Cowboy, the "murderer" in their eyes, to Finney and D'Cenzo.

The submarine crew was known to be one of the tightest knit teams in the Armed Forces, if not *the* tightest. Being submariners themselves, the NIS men couldn't envision the collusion of men committed to one another as a team, to turn around now and submit to the death of one of their own. They knew very well of recent incidents aboard surface craft where greed had produced crime, such as the murder of a disbursing officer in order to steal a payroll. On submarines, the crimes had been mostly misdemeanors, such as petty theft. Never murder! Both Parham and Duvalle had been brought in on domestic affairs where a sailor would steal another man's wife for sex while the husband was on patrol. But to kill your own buddy? Unheard of! Their questioning of D'Cenzo continued.

"A'right, D'Cenzo, spill it! We're on to you. You've repeated Finney's story word for word. Give us the rest of it, from the beginning."

Duvalle was giving him the third degree as he questioned him. He glared at Brains, and was about to grab his collar.

Parham held him back. Duvalle spat out, "You sonofabitch! *You* helped that dumb Texas Cowboy kill your best buddy. They caught him trying to ditch the murder weapon. We're gonna' have your ass!"

For the first time, D'Cenzo heard that Cowboy had been associated with the crime. His mind began to reel. Duvalle had not meant to let him in on Cowboy's suspicious effort to get rid of the .38 from the sub's top deck. D'Cenzo's response, that his friendship with Cowboy was limited, was seen as a ploy and enraged the investigators further.

"Cowboy and I just happen to work on the same boat," said Brains. "We see each other at chow or when we have duty. We don't run in the same circles. I don't know him well enough to even carry on a conversation."

The NIS men now felt he was lying, but after exchanging a note and agreeing, they purposely went to another line of questioning.

"Okay, so you and Cowboy didn't plan this together. Just tell us what happened," was Parham's new and softer approach.

"Yeah," said Duvalle, sarcastically, "how could you and Cowboy have possibly been in on this together?...you hardly knew each other!"

...

New thoughts raced through Brains's mind. Was it too late to implicate Cowboy? In a mini-flash, he considered the possibilities—there was Cowboy's actual superficial friendship, and what Brains saw the NIS feeling: that Cowboy was *the* murderer. He thought further, wondering if he could get a lawyer that would believe a made up story and win him an acquittal. Maybe he would just take the Fifth. He needed time.

Brains kept asking himself why he was protecting the stranger who had actually committed the crime. He was confused.

His day-dreaming about possibilities came to an abrupt halt as

Parham yelled, "Damn it! We've got enough on you and Cowboy to put you up for life. We've had it! We're going to give you five minutes to make a confession."

Parham's abruptness caused Brains to pee in his uniform, enough that he asked if he could go to the head. The NIS were only too happy to comply. They had been hoping for a break, too. They were sure Brains would come back and sign a statement.

...

As Brains left the wardroom under guard, and before the investigators took their head break, Commander Blair broke into the room. Duvalle's coffee went flying as the CO's body slammed into him.

"Oh, God!" he cried out as he noticed D'Cenzo out of the wardroom. "Where's D'Cenzo?" His face had lost its color. "Just got a call from the Med Center CO. They can't find any gunshot wounds on Kozlowzki's body. It looks like a different ball game. Cowboy couldn't have done it!" The NIS men rushed to the officers' head where D'Cenzo had been escorted.

Suddenly over the 1MC came a desperate voice: "Amundsen, Corpsman Amundsen, report to the officer's head immediately." HM1 Amundsen, his medical kit in hand, rushed from his tiny office where he'd been talking to the admin office through the partition window and reached the officers' head in a second. He couldn't believe what he saw.

...

Blood was splashed all over the bulkhead. It was gushing out of Brains's left wrist. The razor blade that he had found was still in his right hand. The guard who had been sent with him couldn't find the pressure point along the inside arm. Amundsen pulled out a rubber tube. Brains had lost too much blood. He lost consciousness. Amundsen stopped the bleeding. He called for a stretcher. The commanding officer and the NIS men stood there, jaws dropped, as they ruffled their hair in disbelief. They looked as Brains's still form, though he seemed to still be breathing.

The sirens could be heard at a distance, and soon the Submarine Base Hospital ambulance was at the head of the pier. *Bluefish* was beginning to look like a ghost of its past. Now it was regurgitating all of its ugliness in one tremendous heave. As Brains rode toward the Submarine Base Medical Center the fluid he had lost was being replaced through IVs.

He could hear the corpsmen, one a woman, whispering, "I think he's going to be all right." He felt her warm hand on his.

He felt giddy and thought, "Oh, hell, maybe I have to be dying to get a taste of heaven."

...

The corpsmen moved swiftly as they wheeled him from the ambulance to the emergency room. As they were rolling him in, a gurney was moving past him. He noticed the sheet covering the body. But the face was uncovered. He winced and let out an audible and painful cry, "My God! It's Tom!"

CHAPTER TWENTY-ONE

BRAINS HAD NOT HEARD from his double date, Candy, since he had ordered a cab to take her to the Groton/New London Airport the Sunday morning that Tom and Rosie were killed.

What had happened, without Brains's knowledge, was that the cabbie had taken her from the Long Hill Apartments to the airport that morning at 5:00 a.m. It was a cold morning. The cabbie saw her hands shaking, and somehow sensed that she was not just shaking from the cold. But what did he know, he was only a cabbie.

As it turned out, she entered the nearly empty, small, but well-maintained terminal. The only ones moving were the USAIR reservations clerk and the two pilots who would take Flight 3484 to Philadelphia.

After catching that flight, she had boarded Northwest Airlines' Flight 683 to Minneapolis. They told her there she'd be in Minot, via Bismark, that afternoon. She hadn't been in Minot since her mother died four years before. She had called her father from Bismark and he agreed to meet her. She couldn't wait to get home. What she had experienced in Groton that morning had made her more nervous than she had ever been.

...

Yolanda Clarissa Stevens—which was Candy's real name—had given Julian D'Cenzo her cell phone number. He had promised to let her know what he'd done with Tom's body. In their fear and desperation, the two young witnesses had agreed to flee and not let anyone know about the ghastly murders in the room next to them, by a stranger. She had an idea that Brains had gone back to *Bluefish* because he had talked about having the duty. As far as she knew, Rosie's body was still back at the apartment.

...

It was Tuesday. She had not heard from Brains. She paced the rooms of the farmhouse where she'd grown up. She spent the time going over and over the events of the past days.

...

Her past was turning in her head. She remembered her mother, Irene, had come down with cancer. The doctor gave her only a few months to live. As a tenth grader she had quit school to help her brother, Tommy, run the dairy. Their father, Clyde, had hurt his back. He spent most of his time in bed, or just sat around. He said it "pained" bad!

It was like living those days all over again. It had been a cold day back then.

She was doing most of the housework. She wished she could move to a warmer part of the country and not have to take care of her little brother. He wouldn't even clean his room. Now, six years later, Tommy was a strapping young man. He and her father, whose back had improved, were in charge of the farm and doing well.

Yolie, as they knew her, had run away just when they needed her. Deep resentment kept them from wanting her around. She had left them with Tommy, a sick mother, and an ailing father. When she'd come back for her mother's funeral two years ago, she had sensed how they felt. It was too late. She had gone back to her new way of life after the funeral.

That first venture into the unknown was still vivid. Friends of hers had told her about warm and sunny Southern California. That sounded ideal compared to North Dakota. She had taken a chance and hitchhiked there. It had been an awful trip. The truck or automobile drivers, no matter what their ages or occupations, made passes at her. She would never do it again. After three miserable days and nights she had arrived in San Diego.

...

All of a sudden, she was awoken from thinking about her past by a dog barking. She saw it was the rural mailman. She kept pacing. The telephone should ring...she thought. She continued to reminisce.

...

The *San Diego Chronicle* carried an ad for an apartment in the North Park area near Balboa Park. A job at an all-night restaurant the day she arrived, and a room at the YWCA had saved her from becoming a homeless teenager who would have joined hundreds of runaways mixed up in drugs and prostitution. The restaurant owner, a woman, had advanced her the required first and last month's rent for the North Park apartment. It hadn't been an easy walk from there to downtown. She liked walking through part of the Balboa Park Zoo. The World's Fair Exhibition buildings were still standing and used to house a variety of businesses and outlets for food, merchandise, and gifts. She, among others, fed the graceful pink flamingos who seemed to wait for her as she gave them bread crumbs.

She had only been sixteen when she arrived in San Diego. She remembered how everyone who heard her story was sympathetic. Young sailors and marines, whom she remembered were plentiful on the main streets of San Diego, were frequent visitors at the Lone Star restaurant where she worked. One of these, a sailor from South Dakota, Jeffrey Redfox, listened intently to her story. It had brought them very close.

...

"Carrot Top" was what she liked to call Jeffrey. He was a big, soft-spoken Midwesterner, with red, almost orange-colored hair. He was awaiting orders in a holding company. Within days of their meeting, Carrot Top had suggested living together. He promised he would pay the rent at Yolanda's apartment. That sounded tempting. He treated her better than anyone in her memory. Seaman Apprentice Jeffrey Redfox, a Sioux Indian from Custer, claimed his mother was Polish. He said his red hair came from her. His skin was ruddy and tanned easily. He wore his uniform with pride and looked impressive. She was sure he was the right person for her. Shortly after they began living together, he got orders to the Naval Training Center at Great Lakes, Illinois. She agreed to go with him even though they weren't married.

...

Yolanda seemed to be in a dream world as she waited for the telephone to ring. *If only the phone would ring!* In the quiet afternoon, she saw her life with Carrot Top pass before her.

A Justice of the Peace had married them after they left the Chicago area. She was eighteen then. Many wives of enlisted Navy men were young. Children abounded. Life was tough, but bearable. At least there were no little ones to eat up the small income they earned. Later, when Jeffrey finished his "A" school and submarine school, they found they were living above their means. Eating out, being entertained, and buying on credit to have "nice" furniture and clothing had left them in the red. The money Yolanda was making at the Pancake House and Jeffrey's pay as a third class petty officer were just not enough. They had qualified to live in Navy Housing at Dolphin Gardens, but they wanted to live in different surroundings. Living there was too much like being on base twenty-four hours a day.

On the same day Jeffrey came home from sub school to announce he'd received orders to a sub out of Holy Loch, Scotland, Yolanda broke the news that she was pregnant. For a brief moment he was very excited. As days went by he never mentioned the coming event, unless Yolanda complained about feeling nauseous. When she attended the sub school graduation, she was the youngest person there. Jeffrey explained to Yolanda about his orders to the gold crew of a ballistic missile submarine, an SSBN. He told her he would be away ninety days at a time, sixty days under the surface of the ocean, standing by for any kind of possible conflict.

It was about that time that Yolanda remembered having problems in their marriage. She remembered that Jeffrey refused to make out an allotment. He said he would provide. He really liked to hear the coins jingle in his pocket and feel the bills fatten his wallet. Sub pay had increased his income, but Yolanda was not informed of the extra pay he was receiving. His division officer and department head counseled all their sailors, but they could not force them to make out an allotment.

He was away for three months and came back for leave and re-training. During the fifth month of her pregnancy she started to go into labor. The OB/GYN on duty was not able to stop the spontaneous abortion. She left the Submarine Base Medical Center depressed and minus the little baby she had so much desired to love. Jeffrey didn't seem to be affected. In fact, he joked about it and told her that at least now they wouldn't have to worry about changing diapers, or getting up at feeding time, or having another mouth to feed.

Jeffrey left soon after his second patrol. He forgot to leave money. As a last resort, she went to Navy Relief, an organization that was set up to help. They made a loan out for her immediate bills. On her way, she stopped at the legal office to see about her right to file for divorce. They told her that under the Soldier, Sailors and Airmen's Act she could not get a divorce while her husband was out to sea. A civilian lawyer took her application. She was going to show Jeffrey who the real boss was in the family!

...

As Candy contemplated her past with Jeffrey Redfox, she knew that filing for divorce had only complicated her life. Pacing the floor, waiting for the phone to ring, she felt tears streaming down her face. The wetness on her cheeks brought her back to the reality that, in fact, the telephone had not rung. It was getting late in the afternoon. How she wished she could lean on someone's shoulder! Thoughts welled up about the disastrous weekend in Groton.

Before that fateful Sunday, Yolanda, now aged twenty and nicknamed "Candy" by her girlfriends, had started to gain weight. People did not see her as pleasantly plump. She always seemed to have a candy bar or box of chocolates within arm's length.

Rosie, along with other girlfriends, had been around to console her after the miscarriage. She had mentioned Jeffrey's apathy to Rosie, who then suggested she better think about filing for divorce.

...

Candy knew that Rosie had divorced three years ago. She had been married to Frank de la Rosa. She told Candy that she finally got tired of being a fisherman's servant. "Rosie" was her nickname. Her real name was Beatriz. She went back to her maiden name, Vieira, and had moved to Groton from Bedford, Massachusetts, a well-known commercial fishing town. She hoped to meet someone new, and living near a military installation seemed to fit the bill.

Rosie had convinced Candy to divorce Carrot Top days before she agreed to double date. Candy had just moved in with Rosie and had told her one night, "You need sex, right? How can you get it when your old man's away—you don't even know where? He may be out there fooling around."

Candy remembered that she and Carrot Top had agreed before that conversation, at his suggestion, that she could fool around as long as he could.

"I may be in Scotland or Italy or France or Spain," he had told her. "I got to have a woman, you know. Wish it was always you, but..."

It didn't make sense, but she wasn't a man and didn't really know that much about sex.

Rosie back then had added, "You can't sit around for ninety days, pure and lily white! Well, you can, but you don't want to wilt away at your age!"

...

Candy's thoughts were interrupted by the ringing of the telephone.

She recognized Brains's voice, weak as it was.

...

Brains was calling Candy from the hospital. His phone was being monitored. The telephone had rung only once. He sensed she'd been waiting nearby for the call.

Three persons were in the hospital room with TM2 Julian D'Cenzo: a corpsman, a member of *Bluefish*'s crew armed with a .45 on orders from the NIS investigators, and Parham, who had rushed behind the ambulance in the NIS official car. Brains had been given permission to make phone calls, but he was told he was under suspicion for the murder or being an accomplice in the killing of TM1 Thomas W. Kozlowski. Brains's left wrist was bandaged as a result of his suicide attempt. He was being given two units of blood intravenously. He spoke while receiving the life-giving substance.

"Hello."

"Candy?"

"Yes...Julian?"

"I can't talk long."

"Just say something."

"I'm in the hospital."

"You're what?"

"In the hospital. I'm under suspicion for Tom's murder. I'm really scared!"

"Oh, no!"

"Where's Rosie?"

"I left her at the apartment."

"Was she dead, too?"

"I guess so. When she didn't talk to me, I got scared and called a cab. It was still dark ...about 4:30 a.m. that Sunday morning."

"No one asked any questions?"

"No. I flew to Minot on the first plane."

"You better come back. We've got some explaining to do."

"I'm scared, Julian!"

"We didn't do anything. I'll have to tell 'em everything. You're an important part of the truth. It'll turn out okay."

"Why are you in the hospital?"

He didn't want to upset her more. "Just routine. I'll be out tomorrow." He knew he was stretching reality.

"Sure?"

"Yeah, just come back. I'm sending you a ticket through a travel agency."

Candy gave Brains her address. Before he hung up, he said, "I saw Tom's body being taken away. The authorities have to check more. Don't say anything to anyone. Call me when you get here. I'll be back on *Bluefish*. If I'm not there, ask for the commanding officer or executive officer. They'll know where I'm at. We might as well come clean about our part."

"Julian. I'm sorry you got messed up in this. You did want to go back to the boat last Saturday. Thanks for the ticket. I'll pay you back."

"Don't worry about that, just get back!"

"Okay, Julian. Goodbye. See ya' soon."

CHAPTER TWENTY-TWO

BRAINS PUT THE RECEIVER DOWN. He asked the investigator if he could call home.

"Go ahead," he said without hesitation. That call, too, was going to be monitored.

When Brains's mother answered, he said in a weak voice, "Mama, just needed to tell you I'm at the Submarine Base Hospital Medical Center. Came in last night. Nothing serious. Just didn't want you to worry in case you found out some other way."

The call came as a shock to his mother. He heard his dad in the background saying, "Iffa that's a Julio, make'a shoor he's a workin' on his degree. Smart'a kid, that!"

"Julio, my boy," said his mother. "What's wrong, son?"

"I'll be fine, Mama. I'll write and tell you."

"Okay, but iffa you need, just'a call."

"Okay, Mama. Love to Dad and all."

"'Bye, bye, son. We love you."

Julian was exhausted. He put the receiver back, closed his eyes and fell asleep. The other three in the room moved into the hall.

Duvalle had joined Parham. They drove down to NIS headquarters on the main street at the sub base and requested New England Bell Telephone Company to let them hear the monitored conversations. They listened intently. The call to Chicago to D'Cenzo's parents said nothing. He sounded like a normal kid wanting to keep his parents informed. They were puzzled. Why wasn't he more nervous about Kozlowski?

The call to Minot was something they found intriguing, to say the least. Who was Candy? Who was Rosie? Where was this apartment where another dead body lay? Why had Candy run away? If neither of them was guilty of murder, why had they not just reported the whole incident to the Groton police? Most puzzling of all, why had Torpedoman Second Class Julian D'Cenzo slashed his wrist? The investigators began to sense this was all beyond their purview.

CHAPTER TWENTY-THREE

ON USS *BLUEFISH* (SSN-645) activity was all but routine. The whole weekend, plus Monday, had been caught up in one bad situation after another. Being out at sea was certainly most peaceful. Tuesday had been another cold and rainy day.

Commander Blair called in his executive officer.

"Ivan, I've just talked to Ensign Palmer. On top of all that's going on, he wants to resign. We don't need this kind of morale problem at this time. What's going on?"

"I told you, Skipper, Palmer's got me all wrong. Okay, I lost my temper with him. I've been trying to keep all the problems of the boat from getting to you. Guess I shouldn't have taken that responsibility."

"I told Palmer I wouldn't accept his resignation. He's primarily pissed off at you for the way he perceives how you handle our sailors, XO," commented CO.

"Well, Thomas's Conscientious Objector application has gotten to him," confessed the executive officer.

Taken aback and shocked, CO queried, "What application?"

"I wasn't going to send it up to you without its being absolutely correct. You me know me and perfection. I think it may be ready. This is the fourth time it's been presented at my level."

He stepped into his stateroom, returned with QM3 Randy K. Thomas's two-inch-thick folder and handed it to the CO. XO's initials indicated he had approved of sending it to the next higher level.

"Well, Ivan, you've been a damn good XO. Can't hold it against you for doing your best. You do need to be more sensitive of the little guy. We'll see if we can't hold on to Palmer. God knows, the Submarine Force can't afford to lose good officers. He's got a lot to learn but he's doing pretty well for a young officer. I just want you to know I'm glad you've been around to absorb the constant barrage. These last few days have topped it all. What do you think'll happen to *Bluefish*, not to speak of Kozlowski's murder?"

Just as he said that, Commander Blair's personal telephone rang. The admin office yeoman buzzed the captain. The yeoman said, "It's the group office. The admiral's on the line."

LCDR Scott was about to excuse himself but the captain said, "Stay!"

"Commander Blair, Washington has just cancelled your orders to be the next executive officer at submarine school. They request you continue as commanding officer *Bluefish* until further notice. They've postponed the in-activation until *Bluefish*'s incidents of this weekend are resolved. I'm sorry about this word. Hang in there. Keep me informed," were the words from squadron headquarters' admiral.

"Yes, sir!" He took a chance that his next question would be understood in the right spirit. "Got anything at all on where they intend to send me?"

"Well...as soon as I hear, I'll let you know. The Pentagon knows you have a fine record. Certainly unblemished until now. Don't know that what has happened will reflect on you. Washington is guarded," he said with hesitation in his voice.

"Thanks, admiral, sir. I'll keep you informed."

Scott could see the disappointment on Phil's face. Haggard lines seemed to appear on his forehead as he put the phone down. He followed the habit of running his hand through his thinning hair. He excused Scott and began to ponder his family's future, but equally important was the future of his crew and USS *Bluefish*.

All plans for de-commissioning had been scrapped for the time being. Life had to go on within the crew of 113 sailors, now cut back by earlier de-commissioning orders to about fifty. An almost complete set of officers—fifteen in number—and technical personnel were left aboard.

The skipper, Jim, was obviously stunned by what had happened to his favorite Sturgeon class submarine, USS *Bluefish* (SSN-645). With all systems still working, they still knew that de-commissioning would take place. It was just a matter of time. Sub Force in Norfolk and the Pentagon would wait.

Among the crew, enlisted and officers, talk about the *Bluefish* and its history was on everyone's lips.

CHAPTER TWENTY-FOUR

THE SUICIDE WATCH TEAM observed every move through the one-way mirror. They had been posted there by NIS. Julian's hand, now tightly bandaged, lay limp across his chest. He knew he had not murdered his friend, Tom.

However, all leads led to Brains, so far as NIS was concerned. Why would anyone try to commit suicide unless they were guilty? It sure added up to that conclusion. But, somehow, there was a question. Part of the inconclusiveness had to do with—why in the world would anyone murder two friends?—and why try to hide the body beneath a submarine? Everything seemed to point away from this sailor, Brains, being the murderer. The NIS were puzzled.

Somehow the involvement of a diving barge and a repair duty sailor from the barge shack added to the puzzlement. But at least they were convinced that the .38 pistol belonged to Cowboy, since he had confessed to owning it.

...

When Candy boarded a plane in Minot, North Dakota, she was filled with the knowledge that Brains, her good friend from *Bluefish*, wanted her by his side. He had told her they had to make sense of all the activities surrounding Tom and Rosie's murders. Brains sounded desperate, and he told Candy she could help clear his name. She sat in her coach seat and tried not to be nervous, but inside she was shaking.

The plane ride into Providence, Rhode Island (actually Warwick, ten miles from Providence), on Northwest Airlines was only five hours away. A plane change in Minneapolis had not delayed her more than half an hour. She arrived in Providence at about 1:30 p.m., and caught a cab. Her father in Minot had slipped her a hundred dollars for the trip.

At 3:30 p.m. she arrived at the submarine base in Groton, Connecticut. Some of the sailors and civilians were already leaving for the day. Plenty of activity was going on.

She asked the cab to wait for her while she got a pass to enter the submarine base.

As he walked into the pass office, the sailor behind the counter asked, "Yes? What can I help you with?" He was a twenty-five-year-old first class sonarman awaiting medical discharge.

Candy, whose buxom figure heaved as she breathed, looked nervous. "I...I...want to visit my good friend. He's a patient at the Medical Center. He called and told me he was there and I...I...I do need to see him desperately."

"Well ma'am," said the sailor, "we can provide a 24-hour pass, but we need to see your identification."

She produced her Connecticut driver's license and had another picture ID showing that she was employed with the Salvation Army. She had been working at the used clothing store on Bank Street for a couple of years. She was glad she had these.

After making copies for their records, the pass office issued a 24-hour pass. She practically ran out of the office and stepped into the waiting cab. The sentry at the main gate was satisfied and waved them on after he glanced at the pass. Once past the gate, the cabbie knew just where to go. He passed the Navy exchange and the commissary, went past the enlisted quarters and parked in front of the Medical Center. After paying the fare, Candy moved quickly into the Center.

Her walk was more like a waddle. The glass doors opened automatically as she approached. After looking right and left, she went straight, to the person behind the information desk. She made it known that she was there to see a patient. There was one person at the reception desk. He was a good-looking third class corpsman. He looked into his computer and found where Brains was. The information on the screen in red letters, with an arrow flashing, indicated that Brains was on "suicide watch." He started to tell her she was not permitted to see the patient.

Candy began to cry! "Please, it's so important! I just came a thousand miles from Minot, North Dakota, especially to see him!"

"Just a minute, ma'am—let me talk to my supervisor."

In less than a minute, a chief corpsman came out and invited her into her office. She broke down again. The corpsman offered her some tissues and, seeing that she looked haggard in spite of her young age, she asked, "Would you like some coffee? Anything else?"

Candy had refused breakfast on the plane, so she was hungry and took the cellophane-covered package of cookies.

While she tried to compose herself and drank the coffee, the chief corpsman investigated how Candy could visit. After what seemed an eternity, the chief returned to the nervous Candy. She was still blubbering and her face was red from crying. She was disheveled and the Kleenex, too, was in shreds.

The chief was wearing a smile! "The *Bluefish* sailor knew you were coming. I found out he had one request by the Naval Investigative Service and they agreed to bring you here, so he called you." She didn't tell Candy that the NIS were hoping for a lead in the murder by having her at Brains's side. "The coast seems clear for you to see Petty Officer D'Cenzo. Before you go, however, we have to do a body search. The reason is," (and it was the first time Candy had heard it), "that your friend Brains is on 'suicide watch.'"

Candy felt goose-bumps up and down her back.

"Are you willing to be searched?" continued the chief.

"Yes...yes...yes! Anything to help my friend. We need to clear things up!"

The chief corpsman didn't suspect the "murder picture." The reasons for Brains's hospitalization were being kept secret.

When nothing was discovered as a result of the total body search, Candy was escorted to Brains's hospital room, leaving her belongings, including her purse, in the chief's office. Walking past the pharmacy and labs and the X-ray department, she proceeded into the elevator to the third floor, down the passageway to the patient rooms. Two Navy men in uniform seemed to be guarding Brains's room—one at each side of the door. One had just moved away from the window where he had looked in on Brains. He was laying sideways on the hospital bed— his arm and wrist were bandaged and an IV tube was hanging from one side of the carrier.

Candy stepped in. Two NIS investigators were in the adjacent room observing through the one-way mirror. A corpsman who was already in the room looked at Candy and motioned for her to move toward the bed. Brains's eyes were closed as though he were sleeping. When she reached over to touch him, he gave a start....opened his eyes and muttered, "Thank God! Candy, this is so very important. Now you can help me!"

NIS listened, watched and recorded every sound.

CHAPTER TWENTY-FIVE

BRAINS TURNED OUT OKAY after his suicide attempt. With Candy at his side, he revealed to NIS what had actually happened that fateful night. Brains talked about his fears and his consequent actions to get rid of Tom's body beneath the sub. The NIS couldn't believe how he had tried to commit a perfect crime. Pepperdine would have never granted a degree even if the crime had been successful.

The investigation by local police had continued, once NIS took over on the side of government involvement. The fact that Tom Kozlowzki was a sailor and was stationed aboard a submarine located within Squadron 25 had moved them to go aboard *Bluefish* to conduct that part of the crime investigation.

When they were convinced the murder had occurred somewhere other than federal property, they were relieved to remove themselves from the case. The murder was definitely a civil case, so the Groton police, aided by the FBI, took over. They waited for the Navy to move.

The murders of Tom and Rosie had indeed been crimes of passion, as the investigators assigned to the case began to surmise.

When Rosie's body was found there were four bullet shots, which had been fired from a weapon aimed at close range. The medical examiner concluded and reported that the four bullet shots had penetrated her body. One was to her vaginal area, one to her torso, scattering part of her chest across the bedroom, both areolae completely blown off. A third shot had been to her neck, where Tom, in moments of lovemaking that fateful night, had left a hickey. And the fourth shot, to complete Rosie's instant death, was between her eyes. The medical examiner confirmed that the shots were all within milliseconds of each other. She now lay in the Groton morgue, awaiting the arrival of someone who would claim her body and begin the burial process, following the appropriate funeral preparations.

The death had been done so quietly that Brains and Candy were not aware of anything happening until they awoke from a deep sleep. The gun to fire the four shots into Rosie had obviously been equipped with a silencer. This explained why Rosie's death went unknown, until she was found later.

The fact that puzzled the investigators was that the body of Tom Kozlowski had no sign of firearm shots from the obviously enraged killer. However, his death gave evidence of an even more mindless murderer.

The killer, who had caught his two victims in a love embrace, showed signs of having premeditated the crime. Tom had not been an easy sight to find in the trunk when Brains got to his ship. The killer had dragged Tom's body to the trunk after taking the keys for the IROC-Z off the kitchen counter, while Brains and Candy slept, totally unaware of the masked intruder's presence. The killer had murmured to himself as he tossed the body into the trunk, "Damn-son-of-a-bitch!" And then he was gone.

When Brains saw Tom's gory body in the trunk of the IROC-Z at the Navy parking lot, blood had coagulated around his chest. The killer had used a knife to penetrate his heart, but there were other signs of butchery. An extremely sharp knife had been used to not only stab Tom in the heart, but to make an incision from his belly-button down through his half-erect penis. It lay cut in two, and the opening of the penis was laid out, glans laid open. It was as if the killer was saying, "Here, you bastard, stick this into the one I wanted only for myself."

When the killer was identified by the FBI through DNA evidence, he turned out to be Frank de La Rosa from Bedford, Massachusetts, Rosie's former husband. He was captured and was awaiting sentence for the first-degree murder of his wife and her lover, Tom.

The days of "gotcha" were over, except for one, the end of *Bluefish* (SSN-645). That, too, would soon take place.

The adventures of *Bluefish*, which closed with days too difficult to imagine, ended with the departure of sailors glad to exit a ship that had gone wrong at the conclusion of an otherwise historic journey.

The Submarine USS *Bluefish* (SSN-645) left its homeport, New London, Connecticut, with a skeleton crew. New London and Groton disappeared in the fog as they sailed away for the last time down the Thames River, into the Long Island Sound and beyond, through the Caribbean Sea, the Atlantic Ocean, through the Panama Canal, and up the Pacific Ocean to Seattle, where *Bluefish* was no longer a war machine. It was cut up and melted down. You may have shaved with it this morning.

ACKNOWLEDGMENTS

I am especially grateful to Richard C. Moore (Dick), whose rendition of art for the cover of this book is more than marvelous.

Thomas G. Schaefer, CAPT, USCG (Ret.) and Clayt Morse, CDR, USN (Ret.), who supplied early advice.

Teresa Balough Peagler and Alice DePret read early accounts on a trip to Israel and Palestine, and supplied encouragement throughout, as did my neighbor Jan Bond, Charlie Sgandurra, a naval history buff, and Norman LaFleur, a poet and Navy veteran who listened with great interest.

Family members such as my sister, Celia, and her husband, Hiram Garcia, let me live in their house in Cochiti, New Mexico when I first started writing this novel, and my adopted father and mother, Elias (Val) and Estela (Mickey) Valdez lent me their typewriter (non-electric) and paper to commence the work.

My wife, Marianne, and our children do much more for my ego by showing their excitement.

I struggled for years, even when the author of *Run Silent, Run Deep*, Edward L. Beach, CAPT, USN (Ret.) discouraged my efforts. In this case reverse psychology kept me moving ahead.

I shall not forget the help given me by Vantage Press—its president, David Lamb, and his colleagues, Wally Swist and my editor, Sharon Pelletier, as well as the designers and copyeditors.

Kudos to Blu-Prints Unlimited, both president Patricia A. Todd and Fallon Matzdorf for a high resolution photo of Moore's original art (cover and back).

There are many whose names are not included in this acknowledgment, but whoever has encouraged me along the way, I thank.

Made in the USA
Lexington, KY
10 April 2014